T0165865

Claire
of the Moon

BY

NICOLE CONN

BELLA
BOOKS
2012

Bella Books, Inc.
P.O. Box 10543
Tallahassee, FL 32302

Printed in the United States of America on acid-free paper
Originally published by Naiad Press 1993
First Bella Books Edition: 2012

Editor: Katherine V. Forrest
Cover Designer: Judy Fellows
ISBN 13: 978-1-59493-327-1

PUBLISHER'S NOTE

The lyrics of the song "Would It Hurt" which appear on pages 129 and 130 are reprinted with the kind permission of the lyricist and composer, Teresa Trull, who created this song for the movie *Claire of the Moon*.

Other Bella Books by Nicole Conn

Elena Undone

When I was in third grade I wrote a short story about pigs. My father thought it held so much promise that he drew up a contract, which I diligently copied in my best handwriting, and he became my agent. Over the years we had many a debate about the realities of being a writer, and on one occasion a battle of wills. Through it all, he had cast his own dreams aside, but never let that stop him from giving me encouragement, approval when I needed it most, and love. This novel, 26 years later, is a testament to our unique bond.

Dedicated to
Daddo
who believed I had talent

Acknowledgments

Many thanks to my family, extended and otherwise, Momo, Beaner, Kate, lil Pookerdoodle, my new niece Lauren, Jennifer, my "number one fan," (and quite the little editor), for keeping me sane while I continue to be a crazy lesbo in LA.

Katherine V. Forrest for her unflagging support, her wise kindness in SF, and her empathy during the "B" factor.

Audra, the woman of my dreams.

I would very much like to acknowledge my wonderful aunt, Carol, who has continued to support me with warmth, sweetness and unconditional love as I continue to follow my unconditional dreams, who let me "live, live, live."

LOS ANGELES

She stood naked at the window. Her body was strong, athletic, what one might almost refer to as masculine in its straightforward approach to the world, but graced with soft curves, full breasts, sprinter's limbs. A full mane of golden brown hair cascaded about her shoulders, down the subtle ridge of her back to the edge of a sheet, draped just above her supple buttocks, wrapped casually about her body as if she were a Greek goddess, out of time, out of place. She was not a generically beautiful woman. But always striking; she was more than a head turner. She drew people in, then often forgot they were there. Her wide-boned face hinted at an Indian heritage, her deeply tanned complexion gave a swarthy and wild appearance when her gray blue eyes courted danger. But when they were still, they cut through ice.

They were deadly at the moment as she surveyed the vast grey brown expanse of a city consumed by car exhaust and human decay. L.A. Hooray for Hollywood.

She lit a cigarette. A man's sinewy form joined her; his hand seductively rubbed the small of her back as he gently extracted the cigarette from her hand and took a drag. She did not turn around or even glance at him as his hand crept up the side of her thigh and traced a line to the swell of her breast. She merely pushed him aside and retrieved her cigarette.

Later she packed. Listlessly. She wasn't sure she really wanted to go to this Writer's Retreat "thang."

"Hey...it'll do you good." She and Ben sat in their normal booth, third down at Kate Mantillini's on Wilshire. Her agent's mouth was full as usual.

"No. It'll do *you* good."

"Babe!" He sported pain like a character out of a bad sitcom. "Don't I always make it right by you?"

"What about Levar?" She watched him inhale his salmon.

"No-o-o-ot."

"Ben!"

"What? I gotta tell ya he's been black-balled? I gotta tell ya no one wants to work with the guy. He's a pain in the frikkin' ass!" He emphasized this last as a piece of spinach salad flew across the table.

"Why, because he's serious? Has some integrity." She poked at her food.

"I told ya. Thinks he's Spike Lee. Sayles. Independent, that's goin' nowhere. Studios wouldn't piss on him if he was on fire." Ben indicated her chicken salad. As his fork swooped in like a bird diving for herring she noticed the stale yellow stains on his thread-worn sleeveless shirt. For an instant a jingle for ring-around-the-collar swept through her mind and she wondered how his wife, Ginny, a wannabe day-timer who could never get anything more than "under-five-lines" no matter how good her last "titter" job had been, as Ben so endearingly referred to it, could tolerate eating opposite this cretin every night, much less go to bed with him. "No money in it, babe. Just leave it to me. Get outta here. L.A.'s so frikkin' hot in the summer anyway." He started in on her bread. "I hear it's pretty nice up there. Relax... find yourself...work on the screenplay—"

"I don't want to work with Ebstein."

"Hey." Ben shrugged defensively. "Babe, you don't wanna work with Levar either. I don't gotta tell ya, ya only climb inta bed with someone who's bigger and bettern' you are."

"You know Ben—" She put down her fork. "That kind of logic is what I love about this whole frikkin' town."

She finished packing. She could always come back. Sure. She could always come back.

OREGON

The Jaguar sped dangerously around the winding coastal curves of the Oregon coastline. The further north she drove, the more rugged the 101 became, the freer she felt. The muscle in her thigh tensed as she pressed the accelerator and whipped around another switchback. She flipped an unlabeled cassette into the stereo and cranked the volume until her body could feel the vibration of the music.

Jazz. Soothe the soul, cleanse the mind. Not the heavy metal rumbling that disturbed her sleep every other night,

her rocker neighbor's incessant need to "express himself."
"White boy's music," her friend Tawny called it. They'd
been having drinks at The Polo Lounge. Tawny was up for
a part in what so many people were gratuitously referring to
as "a small personal film," read low-budget, with the austere
working title *Frantic Illusion*, and they were celebrating
prematurely.

"Look, it's a win-win situation. If I get the part, I can
pay the rent. And if I don't get the part, at least I don't
have to be embarrassed out of this town." Tawny gulped
her wine and motioned the waiter for another round.

"No...I'm fine—"

"Fine my ass. You've been moping around like the
fuckin' plague the last three times I've seen you." Tawny
twisted her straw. "Kevin?"

"Hmmm."

"Kevin." When Tawny didn't get the response she
wanted, "You know, the guy you've been doin' the nasty
with—"

"Tawn...that's over."

"Hmmm...where have I heard that before." Tawny's
tone was sarcastic. "You know what your problem is?"

"No. Perhaps you can enlighten me." She and Tawny
were used to playing pseudo-shrink with one another, glib
and pretentious. The deal between her and Tawny was to
take nothing too seriously so that when they held each
other's hands during the hard stuff they could pretend it
didn't matter.

"You're just not having any fun anymore." Tawny's voice
was serious, and that wasn't playing by the rules. She stared
at the infamously awful Polo Lounge drapes that defined
the rich and famous, then sipped her martini.

****

The frenetic jazz became tiring. Its scaling freedom combined with her escape from L.A. made her anxious. She ejected the tape with frustration. Strains of *Clair de Lune* could be heard through fuzzy, broken reception. She tuned it in and listened, captured by something beyond her immediate vexation. There was a time...but the music crept too dangerously close and she turned it off.

She pulled the Jag into a broad overlook expanding several miles of rugged coastline. She got out, mesmerized. A tarnished rust bled over the swelling waves, jagged rocks and dark blue sky. She stood inert for a long time, then lit a cigarette. She could still turn back. Return to a life that had become the perfect backdrop to her latest best seller: satirical, cynical, and as empty as her last review. She prompted herself to think about the people she must care about. Tawny. Pseudo-friendship she'd never given a chance to be real. Ben was survival. Hordes of "love ya, mean it" acquaintances in the industry. Well, she had "been there, done that." Kevin. A model/waiter from one of her favorite cafes who served double lattes with a smile and charm to go. Great butt. But her heart wasn't in it. Maybe at first. No. She knew that wasn't true. Her heart hadn't been in it for the longest time. Oh, God. She wasn't about to drag that one out. Self-reflection was for self-help groupies who indulged in whining, as she put her idle moments to better use. Even if her heart wasn't in it. Inaction bred ennui. And ennui was not her best "thang."

She threw her cigarette butt to the side, continued to ponder the diminishing blue expanse, then headed for the car.

****

Claire drove through a narrow winding rutted road up to a tarnished cabin surrounded by towering evergreens that, from a hundred years of nor'wester winds, leaned to one side mimicking the Pisa. The relic seemed to sprout from the ground like an enchanted cottage replete with driftwood artifacts, coiling sailor's rope and a large burnt-lettered sign that read *Derriere by the Sea—come sit a spell.* How quaint, she thought, as she gathered her purse with final resolve.

****

"Oh, God...baby...oh, fuck me baby...oh, yes, do it there, that's good—that's sooooo good..." She stopped. Her blue-gray eyes mirrored the reflection of the dimly lit porch light, sparkling with bemused amusement. She was on the second step of the porch leading to what she assumed was her cabin for the duration of her stay at Arcadia Writer's Retreat.

"God, yes, YESSSSSSS!" A man's voice.

"Come for me...Come for me now...show me how much you want it."

Claire's mouth twitched a grin. The noises subsided. She looked around, shook her head, ever so self-consciously, and walked up the stairs to the entrance.

An attractive young woman opened the door. Her preppy chic attire and stylishly coutured French braid were wildly coming apart at the seams. Claire wasn't sure whether to apologize or laugh.

"This is..." Claire began to pull her itinerary from her purse as the young woman waited, somewhat baffled. "Cabin four?"

"Yes." Still breathless.

"May I?" When she didn't get an answer, Claire entered and handed her the envelope as indication she belonged there, then sauntered to the full-length window that framed the wild and untamed majesty of the Oregon coast. The constant rumble of the breaking surf was so close she could almost feel the spray from the aqua-gray waves that mingled with the mist now settling on the battle-scarred foliage.

"Oh yes...yes...that's it...that's the way... right there, now, right there ..." The voices started up from a back room, but they were distinctly two women this time. Claire turned to the woman who seemed as startled by the noises as Claire.

"Am I...interrupting?"

But before she could answer a strong, compelling voice from another room barked, "Amy, I can't do this by myself you know."

A tall striking woman, with classic aquiline features that matched her perfectly tailored Heather tweed and crisp maroon oxford shirt, appeared out of the cries of lust. Her short-cropped auburn-brown hair fell softly about her face emphasizing the squareness of her jaw. She had intense brown eyes that would pierce the mundane. She halted when she saw Claire.

"Oh...I'm sorry." She glanced at Amy. "I didn't know we had company."

Amy uncertainly presented Claire. "Dr. Benedict, I believe this is your, uh...roommate."

The tall woman graciously extended her hand. Claire shook it apprehensively, but immediately extracted her own when the anguished moaning resumed.

"I'll get it." Amy rushed by Dr. Benedict, who appeared somewhat at a loss for words, then awkwardly explained, "Research."

Amy returned, seemingly miffed. "That damn VCR!"

Claire smiled for the first time, finally understanding.

"Noe—uh, Dr. Benedict," Amy offered, "why don't I get another one. I could bring it down Monday."

"I don't think the VCR is the problem."

"Really, I could take this one back—"

"That's quite all right, Amy—"

"It's just that I don't want your work interrupted." Amy paused, proud and enthusiastic as she beamed from Dr. Benedict to Claire. "*Ms* is devoting an entire segment to Dr. Benedict's theory on the relationship of pornography to intimacy."

"I didn't know they were related," Claire mused.

"Distant cousins," Noel responded. "From opposite sides of the closet."

Claire reassessed the doctor, and smiled. Dr. Benedict glanced at the floor, suddenly appearing somewhat shy. Claire was surprised; shyness was not a characteristic she would have attributed to the self-possessed doctor.

"Well, I better get back to it." Her smile was brief, dismissive as she returned to the room of electronic research.

****

She found his picture lurking beneath the debris of her unpacking. That last afternoon she had attempted to listen as he recited the lines from a commercial for hair coloring.

"Kevin, don't you think it's a tad ludicrous to have someone your age playing the part of a graying fifty-year-old?"

"Hey, I'm sensitive. What can I say."

"No. You're young. And they expect the rest of the male population will assume they'll look as sensitive as you if they glop enough of their hair toner on."

Kevin wasn't listening. He was too busy preening, but when he finished he strolled over to her with a cocky grin. "Lighten up, babe. I still got twenty minutes." He wrestled her to the couch, kissed her right breast.

She pushed him away, got up and moved to the dresser. On her way she picked up his second-hand Armani silk shirt and threw it at him, indicating their time was at an end.

"Ya know, Claire. Sometimes you act like you're about a thousand goddamn years old," he moaned as he reluctantly put on his shirt.

She walked to the window, then, more to herself than anyone else, whispered, "I am."

Claire studied the head shot he'd stuck in her suitcase as a romantic gesture. Curly blond hair, curly blond brains. She shook her head as she dumped it into the waste can on her way out of her new bedroom.

****

"Are you sure?" Claire overheard Amy's eager voice. "I can get a place nearby. There's still so much to do on the surveys."

Claire had strolled from her bedroom, which faced north toward the majestic Haystack Rock—icon and hot tourist spot—to explore the interior of the living room/kitchenette of weather-worn cabin four, softly lit by two restored oil-lamps. Mysterious shadows were cast from tokens that lined the built-in bookshelves, yesteryear's strolls by the beach, a myriad of shells, driftwood, treasures swept up along the tide, and sand dollars wedged between ragged paperback bestsellers for readers with a more discriminating taste. Claire saw *The Naked Truth*, by Dr. Noel Benedict, propped against a framed photo of what appeared to be an older man, perhaps her brother, bundled in a pea-coat with his arm around her new cabin-mate. Upon closer inspection she realized it was a woman, yes...the woman who ran the retreat. She recognized her now. Definitely a beach relic. She was about to pick up the hardback tome when she heard Noel responding to Amy, her voice strengthening as the two women approached the living room.

"Amy. It can wait until I get back. Now, I want you to go. Before it gets dark—"

"Noel—" Amy's voice was pleading. Then she was blushing as she realized there was another person in the living room. Claire ambled to the window trying to catch the outline of the waves through the fading light.

"And don't forget to ring Sam when you get back to town," Noel said as she steered Amy to the front door.

Amy seemed unwilling to budge. "Well..." she grappled,

"... have fun. I guess." She peered at Claire suspiciously. "If I finish collating the reports—"

"Amy—don't worry about it. Thanks for your help." Noel maneuvered Amy out the door before she could say another word, closed it and turned around with a frustrated sigh.

Claire turned from the window. "Sounds eager."

"She's brilliant—but too goddamn much energy."

Claire smiled, and followed that with a stiff silence.

"You're from L.A.?" Noel asked.

"Hmmm...but only bred there. Self-made nouveau chic." Claire felt slightly defensive. She thought how she must appear in what she referred to as The Uniform; faded holey jeans, a white T-shirt with the inscription, *Give Me Coffee And No One Gets Hurt*, covered by an oversized, black tailored blazer rolled at the sleeves, complete with her black shit-stomping boots. "And you...you're from...

"Portland."

"Beautiful city."

"If you don't mind the rain."

Claire stared out at the ocean. "I adore gloomy days."

Silence.

Noel said, "I've...uh...heard your name, but I don't believe I'm familiar with your work—"

"Dr. Benedict—"

"Noel."

"Noel. You know, I'm really lousy at small talk."

"Yes." Noel leaned against a worn mahogany hutch that housed additional sentimental beach memories, old photos and an antique blue and white Wedgwood tea service with one cup missing. "I suppose it does seem rather absurd when we'll be spending the next month together."

"Yeah." Claire strolled to the refrigerator, removed a bottle of Chardonnay. "Anyway, don't take it personally." Claire held up the bottle in invitation. Noel declined with a head shake. "It's just...chit chat bores the tits off me."

****

Claire's body moved seductively to the rhythm of a sensual ballad as she put the finishing touches to her fingernails. Paris, a black model who had made it big on Italian runways, had told her once, over double cappuccinos, that she possessed the compelling trait of self-assurance. There was no more attractive trait, he pronounced with utter conviction as he gracefully lit her cigarette. Self-assurance directly led to power. He should know. He was on his way. Paris had taught her a lot back in those days, when they were both struggling. Now that they had made it, they didn't see much of each other anymore.

Claire pumped up the volume. She remembered the last time they had gone dancing. Catch 1. Hot. Humid. Sweat-gritted floors as she and Paris swayed rhythmically to the incessant pounding of the generic club beat. He was teaching her the latest in Eurocool club moves. Tall, handsome, glistening Paris gliding with the grace of a modern Adonis. She appreciated him on an aesthetic level. But what she really found intriguing was the woman in the corner, who danced by herself. Her white tank top contrasted with her dark olive Hispanic skin, and her body was fluid, sensual, inviting. Claire was a little drunk. She wanted to dance with her, but something held her back.

She knew now that she had been intimidated. An emotion she rarely experienced. Now the woman's body floated dangerously near...

"Excuse me!"

Claire jumped from her reverie.

"Excuse me—"

Claire turned down the music.

Noel towered above her. "I never was any good with loud music."

"Sorry...I thought you had left."

"No."

Claire twisted the cap onto the nail polish bottle. Noel was looking at the discarded cotton balls, nail file, paraphernalia of the vain, cluttering the dining room table. "Well...I should get back to it." She began to retreat.

"Unless you want to tag along tonight." Claire was flip. "I thought I'd check out the local color."

"Thanks, but—"

"You're dedicated, upright and disciplined." Claire sighed for effect. "So am I. Can you believe it? But...only when the mood strikes *me*."

Recognition lit Noel's eyes. "That's it. You wrote *Life Can Ruin Your Hair*."

"Yeah." Claire's enthusiasm was hardly over-whelming.

"Yes. I saw you on Oprah."

"Sells copy." Claire was defensive. "Did...you read it?"

Noel shook her head.

"No. No it wouldn't be your genre."

"Great title."

"It was appropriate at the time." Claire lit a cigarette, and said, her voice adopting an insinuating tone. "I was deeply miserable at therapy."

"It has been known to have that effect." She stared at the smoke rising from the cigarette.

Claire took a deep drag. Not taking her eyes off Noel, she went to the ceiling fan and pulled the chain. They merely stared at one another as the blades went round and round until Noel backed down and left the room.

****

The vigorous twirling of a spoon in a teacup splintered the silence of the still, blue dawn. Noel peered out the center of the large picture window at the very spot Claire had occupied the day before. She gazed out at the ocean, caught by its infinity, its never-ending possibilities, its evocation of memories. She took a delicate sip of tea.

"Do you always drink tea?" The voice still haunted. The exact timbre, the tone...the eyes, skin, taste. All of it, flooding over her, her senses assaulted, until she felt she could actually smell the light muskiness of chamomile lotion mixed with sweat on Erika's softly flushed skin after she had worked out.

Noel had been attending a conference on panic disorder. A gray-clad colleague's abysmal approach to desensitization droned endlessly; a certain cure for insomnia. She sureptitiously slipped from the last row of the Southend Suite in desperate search for the cafeteria and Earl Grey. As she paid the cashier, the woman with the cashmere sweater and leather brown skirt whispered behind her, "Tea. Every break."

"Not always. Mostly." She had been so deeply immersed in her own approach to the previous topic discussed, it took her a moment to get her bearings.

"Was a bit tedious, wasn't it?"

Noel detected a faint accent. Not quite British, but a hybrid mixture of back east and abroad. She wasn't in the habit of judging academics on performance but she did not want to appear rude. "Yes, I suppose it was."

The brunette extended her hand. "Erika. Erika Morgenstern."

"Noel Benedict."

"Yes. I heard your dissertation on intimacy."

"And how did I rate?"

Erika Morgenstern's eyes brimmed with electricity. "Oh...very well. In fact—" Erika Morgenstern leaned to throw her Sweet 'n Low into the trash, her soft shoulder-length hair just brushing Noel's cheek. "I'd like very much to hear more."

Noel shivered as she felt the chill in the cabin. She pulled her flannel robe tight, continued to stare out at the breaking waves and took another sip of tea, hoping it would thaw the chill inside.

****

Claire stumbled out of her bedroom into the kitchen lazily clad in a maroon pin-striped robe she had picked up at an estate sale in San Francisco. It looked like something out of an old Clark Gable movie, was far too large but she loved the silk against her nude body. Her hair tumbled carelessly about her shoulders as she knocked around the cupboards and freezer searching for one thing, and one thing only.

Then she searched diligently for a grinder. Rotely and without regard to her surroundings she dumped the dregs of some long lost Colombian beans in the grinder and pulverized them to a fine, silt-like powder. Dripping a trail of water behind her, Claire clumsily plopped the kettle on the burner and turned it to high.

"You're up," Noel not so politely inferred.

Claire jumped. She had no idea how long Noel had been standing there. "I'm...upright." The air lay still between them. "Uh...did the noise bother you?"

"I was about to take a break." Polite.

"Been at it long?" Nonchalant. Claire took a moment and glanced with pseudo-interest Noel's way. Her impeccable attire was perfect for the tightened shoulders, the stress-lined jaw of someone who was taking her work entirely too seriously.

"Since five."

"Jesus! That's obscene." It came out before Claire could stop herself. The steam whistled. Round One, to the sloppy blonde in the corner.

Noel began to walk away, but then stopped and threw over her shoulder, "Perhaps you might grind your coffee at night."

Maggie gazed at the rather motley group of eight women for whom she would play hostess, housemother and confidante over the next four weeks. They lounged informally in her spacious living room that contained her favorite memories, some best left forgotten. History. The place had history and character. Even if there was need for a little repair here and there. It hadn't escaped her that it was more work and less fun. Just couldn't keep up the way she used to. Even that poor damn piano needed tuning. But she had her bears. Polar bears. Twenty original polar prints. Painted them herself, and they were damn good if she didn't say so herself. The rest of them...the stuff her friends gave her, all those silly little polar bear gee-gaws, salt and pepper shakers for christsakes...well, it was just plain goofy, but what the hell.

"So...if there's anything you need, just bellow." She

scanned the eight faces. Oh, Jesus, this was going to be good. Thank goddess Noel was here. And, of course, her dear BJ. "But make it in the afternoons. I'm a late riser." She watched Noel and the blonde exchange looks and then sever contact simultaneously. Maybe sticking them in Cabin Four hadn't been such a good idea, after all.

"All the cottages on the east side are retreat cottages," Maggie continued. "The others are private. This is our tenth year and most of the locals know we're just a bunch of crazy broads writing our guts out, trying to find the meaning of life."

"Anything of cultural merit in town?" Adrienne was a reed-thin, straight-backed poet from New York. Her esoteric haikus had been the rage last year and when she had applied Maggie thought the publicity might do the writer's retreat some good.

"Yes. Do tell," a soft chubby southern voice chimed in. It belonged to a rather campy and plumper version of Blanche DuBois.

"If you want recreation, you'll find it at the Humpwhale Inn, along with Hemingwayesque provincialism. Plenty of stories there, and..." Maggie peered at them warningly, "... trouble. As for culture—" She strolled towards Adrienne. "If you're talking about Broadway plays, you can forget it. But they have a great bookstore, damn good local theater, and hey...plenty of fresh air."

"Just what I aspire to." Adrienne sighed.

"Try and remember, when you're having one of those blocks, girls, we are here to work."

"All work and no play—" the southern belle intimated.

"—usually gets published!" Maggie dismissed her and walked to the front of the fireplace where she grabbed her beer. She watched their reactions. This was the first year the retreat hadn't maintained a theme. But after last year with all those crazy sci-fi chicks running around the place,

Maggie had lost it with their ramblings, their runaway imaginations concocting the ultimate in ookey-pookey! Where did they come up with that stuff? And the year before that—eighteenth century poets. Get thee a life! So let's just throw them all in together, add water, stir 'em up... see what develops.

Maggie's favorite pastime, next to sipping a vintage Bordeaux, was studying human behavior, and though she had become a bit dispirited about the human race on the whole, she still believed that every single soul on the planet had some good, even if it might only be half a kernel. And, every so often she was still surprised. Like by this mix. There couldn't possibly be a more incongruous group. The blonde. She was the one to watch. Very to herself. Very L.A. Kneeling next to her, Indian style, was a woman who was either brave or bizarre enough to wear a tie-dyed cotton rainbow dress with black leggings and a yellow scarf wrapped around her frail mid-section. BJ sat between her and the housewife from hell, whom BJ had insisted she allow into the group against Maggie's better judgment...some long lost friend of a cousin who thought it would be good for her. And then the damn poet and the silly southern thing. Of course, Noel was imitable. Noel and Maggie found a great deal of comfort in that.

Maggie took a sip of her beer and then continued with her pat speech. "If you need a sounding board for plot, theme, what the hell you were writing about in the first place, I'll gladly lend an ear. Or you can use each other. Tuesday and Thursday nights are the infamous 'trash' meets...discussions on everything from syntax to Playtex. Optional of course, but I'll tell ya, everyone starts to look forward to them..." Maggie continued, mockingly melodramatic, "...after the lonely solitary hours of neverending toil."

Well! That about wraps up this initiation thing. Any questions?

The women glanced about themselves with anywhere from blank to amused expressions on their faces. Maggie sidled over to Noel. The southern belle and Adrienne gathered around the shy slinking naturopath, Shilo Starbright, who was writing a book on the history of herbal medicines. Lynn, the young but ragged housewife, aspiring to science fiction—probably because she lived it, Maggie thought not unkindly—stood quietly on the fringes blocked by the sheer presence of the grand dame of pulp fiction, Miss Tara O'Hara. Noel and Maggie spoke in low tones as they leaned over the large stone hearth several feet away.

"Quite a gathering you've collected here," Noel commented. Maggie watched her eyes follow the blonde who was sharing a brief exchange with her very own BJ Thornton. Ah, Beej...what a woman. You would never know she was a well-known historian. She was too sexy to belong to the halls of academia, and those eyes, as wise and lively as they were kind and sincere. And sexy. Damn sexy.

"Why...why it's Claire Jabrowski!" The southern belle intercepted her. "Tara. Tara O'Hara!" The blonde did not recognize her. "From the writer's convention in Atlanta!"

"Yes. How could I forget." Cheeky reply, but then she carried it off, as Maggie guessed she usually did.

"Well. I'd never expect to find you up here in the wilderness. After L.A. an' all." Tara winked as if they shared exclusive sophistication.

Claire looked at her wearily. "One jungle's as good as the next."

"I—I've read every one of your books." Lynn boldly stepped forward and then shrank back. "I...I really love them."

"Thanks." Claire smiled with genuine pleasure then caught Noel and Maggie observing them, and her face changed as if she had been caught taking part in a social experiment.

"Adrienne King." The poet extended a lanky limb.

"Shilo—"

"—Shilo Starbright," Tara finished for her. "Isn't it fascinatin' how these holistic types come up with such conceptual names."

"Unlike your own."

Tara completely missed the jibe as Claire extended her hand to Shilo and then Lynn.

"Lynn Schroeder." Maggie couldn't figure out if she felt sorry for this miscast character among this band of what she suspected could be rapier-edged conversationalists. Maybe the experience would somehow strengthen the backbone of this Stepford housewife whose fragility seemed more a result of haggard abuse than inherent weakness. "I'm so thrilled to be here. I've never...well, that is, I've got a short story published...but really, to be in the company of so many celebrities," she fairly gushed, "This is...great!" she whispered loudly to Tara.

Maggie leaned to Noel. "Sorry to leave you to your own devices, but I'm in dire need of refreshment." Another beer would help her endure the rest of this prattle. As she passed the huddle she heard Lynn gasp, "Isn't that.. . oh, the tall one, leaning by the fireplace—"

"Noel Benedict. Dahk-tah of lu-u-uv." Tara pulled Claire conspiratorially to her side. "I haven't read *The Naked Truth* myself, but from reliable sources I hear she lets it all hang. Simply every which way." Tara sighed for emphasis. "Personally I think she's a frustrated eunuch."

"I think you have the wrong term," Claire corrected. "Eunuch describes a castrated man."

"Well, I always say, if the shoe fits."

Claire studied Noel, confused by Tara's inference.

Tara resumed self-importantly. "She's not just your run of the mill 'sex-therapist' on the talk-show circuit, ya know. She's a ravin—"

"Excuse me." Claire cut her short as she did the contact with Noel.

Maggie watched her make her escape. She also watched Noel, whose eyes followed her every movement.

She watched her toes in the bathtub, the steaming water almost burning her as it gushed around them. When she could no longer bear the heat she extended her leg, and then her toe to twist the HOT faucet handle off. She soaked. Numb. The hot water made her feet itch, but the delicious pain could not ease the swollen thing that had become her heart.

Apathetically she swirled the water about her breasts, then stretched her arm before her as if pulling beads of water in solid form, scrutinizing them as they plopped into the surface, forming perfect round smoke rings of liquid. She stopped suddenly and stared at her hand. She studied it for a very long time. A tear rolled down her cheek.

She had been sitting just so for an hour. If she thought about when it was good, the pain struck, as if she might have a heart attack. A heart-ache attack. It began slowly, a nagging sensation that could be swished away like an annoying gnat, but, like the incessant rumbling of traffic below her office when she most needed to concentrate, the pain became more noticeable. And then came the words. All the words. They had both promised. Forever.

She sighed. It never went away. Like an emotional neuron spiraling around its mother atom. And then there was another memory whirling towards her from some outlandish association and pretty soon all the memories and electrons and neurons whirled around her heart and made her want to choke.

But she cried instead. Silently. She wasn't sure if her muffled sounds could be heard by what she now felt was an interloper. After all, last year she and Erika had spent nothing less than a magical month together here...even if it was hidden away from the world, reality. And why did she have to agonize over her now, when she had so clearly dealt with this months ago? Why now?

Should she apply a new theory to delayed trauma syndrome? Could you do that with everything, she wondered. Like programming the VCR. Eight events at a time. My, how progressive.

This delayed pain was cruel. It beat on you when you least expected it. Even for someone who played games on pain with her patients. Controlled, and contained, willing pain away by simply intellectualizing its departure. But what about the unexpected? Those moments you have no control over? The minute she smelled the ocean air, its briny traces recalling every moment they had walked hand in hand by the water's edge, the snap in the air, the slant of the sun as it fell against the carpet where they had made love long into the afternoon. And music. She couldn't listen to any of her favorite music. Restaurants, movies, TV shows. Anything you did together became masochistic indulgence.

Her toes were wrinkling. She observed this with the detached professionalism she utilized with all her patients.

Victims of grief, pain, abuse, and never-ending horror stories of the human condition. Every cell on her skin was waterlogged. Water therapy. She had recommended it a number of times. Water therapy as a compromise to liquid abuse. She would rather be soaking in a tub of bourbon. Now all she could do was stare at the rubbery skin that slipped and slithered into grotesque forms as her tears came faster and fuller. They slid down her cheeks, dropped on her breasts, salted tributaries into deadened grey water.

She screamed.

Silently.

****

Claire stumbled into the kitchen, grabbed the coffee beans, pried the lid carelessly from the grinder. Pre-ground coffee scattered the countertops and covered her from nearly head to toe. When she got her bearings, the deduction sank in. She cocked her head towards Noel's room, more than irritated, as she slammed the grinder back on the counter. Round Two goes to the stalwart Dr. Benedict. It took every effort on her part not to storm in and assert her rights to the kitchen. Something held her back. And then a mischievous smile fell over her face. This was definitely the beginning of war.

****

Noel studied the pages before her, wondering if she was more upset with the content of the material—the cruel statistics of the nation's obsession with the pornographic visual medium—or her inability to concentrate. She had spent one month for each of the last five years in this cabin, primarily isolated with her work. Regardless of the group of writers, Maggie had kept this particular cabin for her annual vacation. But Maggie hadn't gotten around to repairing the plumbing in the cabin next to hers and she was the one suffering the consequences. Her privacy was paramount to her, not only because she was a private person, but because she did her best work alone. Now she was too clearly aware of another's movements. This cabin was too intimate. That and those damn cigarettes. Foreign. They might be the height of fashion in L.A. but they were nothing more than a rude intrusion to her.

She turned to stare at the artwork she had brought here a few years back, left in this south room of the cabin for Maggie and others to share. It gave her a sense of self. She could lose herself in the complex, textured nudes, appreciating the bold and individual style of the artist, an ex-patient, who had very little money but a great deal of talent. Noel had treated her for free and had been gifted with these rare pieces in exchange; the better end of the deal. They usually provided her with a great deal of comfort, but as Claire's cigarette smoke got thicker, Noel found it difficult to feel at peace.

Noel got up and walked to the living room. Claire sat at the couch staring at the screen of her laptop. She groped with one hand and lit a cigarette, unaware she already had one going, completely focused on the task at hand. Noel shook her head, then found herself momentarily taken back by Claire's nonchalant appearance. Her hair was casually and sensually pulled back. She was clad in a loose fitting white tank top and holey jeans, another fashion statement that lent more farm girl innocence than an air of sophistication as Claire tackled her work in this rural setting. Smoke swirled furiously about her as she gulped coffee that appeared to have been sitting there for hours, followed by an intense drag from her cigarette. Noel was jolted into her reasons for disrupting her own work in the first place.

"Excuse me."

Claire continued typing.

"Excuse me! Is it quite necessary to have two going at the same time?"

Claire merely ground the cigarette in the ashtray, and continued typing.

Noel was about to continue but Claire put her hand up. "I am really focused here. Can it wait until later?"

Frustrated and recognizing a roadblock when she ran into one, Noel exhaled loudly and returned to her room.

****

"Where are you?" Maggie studied her good friend's face. It was hard for her to look at the raw pain. It infuriated her because she knew there was nothing she could do about it.

"Hmmm?"

Maggie poured the final dregs of a rare Cabernet into Noel's wineglass. "Shall I call in the local exorcist?"

Noel shook her head gently, stared into the fire. Her jaw tightened, the muscles rippling her fine-lined face. "Sorry."

"Don't be. Just remember, darlin', never-ending agony is so addictive."

"I'm over it Maggie. Really."

"You're full of shit. Besides it's so alluring on you, Noel. The mysterious therapist who made brooding a fine art. And for what?" Maggie's voice was acerbic. "Definitely not the 'objet de passion.'" She sighed plaintively over a sip of wine, trying to figure out how best to soothe this woman with whom she shared an uncommon but binding friendship.

Five years now. And though they seldom saw one another, her connection to this fine woman was one of the closest she had ever allowed herself.

It had begun in Boston. One of the rare occasions she

traveled anymore. An old pal had died from AIDS. She had lost many friends and her anger was bubbling just beneath the surface. She needed a drink. Or two. She had taken a cab to the Park Plaza Hotel, marveling at the city's ability to wed modern architecture to the gentrification of proud old Boston. She had gotten out, lit up a cigarette, and noticed a man lying, face down, in the flower patch by the bus stop. She looked around. People passed by, so caught up in their own worlds they didn't see or didn't care. Maggie rushed over in the same instant a tall, slender jogger knelt by the man's side and carefully picked up his wrist to check for a pulse. The jogger authoritatively took charge, commanded one of the minimally gathering crowd to call an ambulance as Maggie covered the man with her thread-worn pea-coat. The woman loosened his tie and stood up. Only she and Maggie remained until the ambulance arrived and packed him in. He had suffered a mild seizure. When the lights flashed and the siren boomed its way through traffic, Maggie and the woman shared a relieved smile.

"May I buy you a drink?" Maggie definitely needed one by this point.

"I think we deserve it."

"And doesn't it mean if you save someone's life with a perfect stranger that you, I don't know, have to marry each other's second cousins or something..."

It broke the tension. The woman laughed a wonderful laugh that filled her eyes and broke the sternness of her jaw. They made their way to Cheers and spent the rest of the afternoon and evening examining their own lives through each other's eyes, veritable strangers, given permission to unlock doors by the bizarre machinations of circumstance.

Maggie watched Noel attempt to cover a single tear that escaped her brimming eyes. "Obsessing over something you can't have is the biggest turn-on." Her voice was gentle. "You crave passion like you're sniffin' it up your nose. And possession, ah...nine-tenths of nothing. It never existed, Noel."

"Maggie." Noel's voice was affectionate. "You're such a goddamn pain in the ass when you play shrink."

"But I'm such a lovable pain in the ass."

Maggie poked at the fire, sat back and tried yet another tack. "Dating?"

"Not seriously."

"Sleeping around."

"Oh...occasionally...and cautiously."

"But no one—"

"Maggie! What in the hell possessed you to put that woman in my cabin?"

Maggie responded rather sheepishly. "Hmmm... I was wondering when you were going to get around to that."

"What were you thinking?"

"I thought she'd be good for you. Get you out of yourself...Maybe...I don't know—"

"She's...she's rude. Disorganized. Cluttered. She smokes like a truck driver. And...she's so..." Noel searched for the definitive adjective. ". . . straight."

"But interesting."

"About as interesting as a black widow."

"Dangerous, huh?" Maggie took great delight in egging her on.

"Intolerable."

Maggie's eyes were a mixture of genuine sweetness and condescending wisdom. She took another sip of wine. "I knew you'd like her."

****

Noel had to smile, even though she was irked with Maggie's transparent little scheme to break her from her idyllic memories and longing for Erika. She meandered down the steep and eroding path to the beach with renewed respect for mother nature. In one year the raging winds and shifting tides had almost made it unnavigable. And Maggie seemed less able to repair or simply less inclined. Dear, dear Maggie. Such a sweet curmudgeonly enigma; short and compact, cutting a dashing if somewhat dated figure in her Birkenstocks, red flannel shirt and jeans. She might be mistaken for a throwback, but there was clear intelligence in her eyes, and she was still a very handsome relic in her forty-seventh year. However, her well-intentioned friend's maneuver of ameliorating loneliness with someone as aggravating as her cabin-mate would not be her own first avenue of remedies as a therapist. It was simply going to take time. Time. God, why did it always have to take so much time? Healer of all evils.

The cool air felt good. She was still a bit lightheaded from the wine. Maybe a moonlight stroll on the beach would clear it. She needed a good night's rest if she ever hoped to get any work done.

Noel wound her way to the beach. The tide was low and calm as she walked along the rippling ebb.

"It doesn't have to be over." She had stood in her office overlooking the expanse of lights glittering in the deep blue of dusk and reflecting magically off the Willamette River. Her city. She towered above it and the rest of humanity in her professionally austere cubicle, with the most beautiful view a lease could buy, protected from those stick figures that buzzed about twenty-six floors below, and now from the woman who floated somewhere behind her. If she turned around it wouldn't be over. The shadow of the woman moved toward her, put a hand out to Noel's shoulder.

From the moment they had laid eyes on each other that weekend they were inseparable. Noel always had very little use for the term "love at first sight," having been inundated by never-ending tales of woe that particular phenomenon had caused in the larger part of her client base. She had never bought the contrived romanticism that flooded American culture, and having only once been infatuated, she considered herself immune to vagaries of the heart. But when those eyes captured her own in the small Italian restaurant she and Erika had escaped to, Noel discovered an altogether new reaction to feminine beauty. And it had very little to do with clear or rational thought.

They barely touched the vegetarian lasagna. Dabbling over Tiramisu and brandy, Noel was amazed by the freshness and unusual capacity for light this woman brought to the table. In their mutual profession conversation tended towards shop. But not with Erika. Erika had no interest in discussing anything but Noel and her life, dreams and desires. It wasn't until the weekend was over that Noel discovered Erika wasn't in the profession. Merely interested.

That first night had been unlike anything Noel had ever experienced. She had been aware for several years, with clinical detachment, that she was a lesbian. She had slept with two women up to that point. One as an experiment and the other as a possibility for a relationship. They were great friends but lousy lovers. Erika was simply the most exquisite thing that ever happened to Noel's sexuality. There wasn't one part of Erika's well-proportioned hard-won physicality that didn't arouse her. She loved every smell and taste that was Erika.

Noel closed her eyes with a long expired sigh. The face floated before her, once again. She could either exorcise the delicate features and go to bed, or she could entertain them in the blurred edges of reality. She would anyway, in her dreams.

This was hopeless. Noel followed the path back to her cabin. She had to stop the memories prying beneath her contained surface, unlocking battle scars that would do nothing but impede her progress. She knew all this stuff. She knew it until she was sick to death of it. Theory and practice were the oddest of bedmates when they were clearly the worst kind of strangers.

She opened the door. The cabin was dark and she could barely make out the shadows of the furniture. But as she edged forward the smoke from Claire's cigarette caressed the moonlight where she knelt at the bench by the window.

They exchanged a brief glance, then Noel made an abrupt move to her room.

"Noel?"

Noel stopped.

"I'm...sorry. I mean about earlier."

Noel turned, surprised by the warmth in Claire's voice. "It's...no problem."

"Well, it is actually. I...I get so...nothing else exists. I'm not used to co-habiting." Claire took a drag from her cigarette. "This is heaven."

Noel relaxed then, enough to join Claire at the window. The moon cast a shimmery glow to the soft waves. "The most beautiful place on earth."

"It's difficult. Isn't it?"

"Hmmm?" Noel didn't follow.

Claire took a long drag off her cigarette, let the smoke rest in her lungs then exhaled with a noticeable amount of frustration. Silence rested between them until Claire's jaws tightened ever so lightly and she finished with mild irony, "Sharing paradise with a stranger."

****

Sweaty, grimy, and breathless from her run, Claire clumped in, throwing off her sweatshirt as Noel boiled water for tea. They politely acknowledged one another's existence, and Claire wandered to her room. When she returned seconds later sweat glistened on her nearly unclad body.

Noel did not consider herself overly modest but Claire's black bikini sportswear with a towel barely draped over her shoulders made her feel exposed herself. She turned inward, occupying herself with the quiet tradition of making tea. As Claire assertively pulled a beer from the refrigerator Noel was reminded of the quintessential bull in a china shop.

Claire said, "I'm taking a shower."

"There's not much time before the meeting."

"What meeting?"

"The Tuesday night meeting."

"Oh that."

Claire swigged her beer.

"You're not going."

"No. But let me guess. You are."

"Yes."

Claire appeared amused as she began to unravel her braid. "I bet you fill out warranty information."

Noel refused to be baited even if something about this conversation made her feel like a prude. "I have no use for warranties...but I do for other people's ideas."

"So do I." And then Claire added somewhat defensively, "I'm just not the Kaffee Klatsch type."

"And you have someplace better to be."

"Ohhhh...I dunno. Humpwhale Inn sounds a bit inbred to me, but hey, who knows."

Noel contemplated Claire in silence while she fidgeted with her bottle. "I can't wait until tomorrow to hear what I missed," Noel said dismissively as she left the kitchen.

Claire watched her retreating figure, then took a long swallow of beer as she stared out to the ocean. She just wasn't going to let this uptight anal shrink get to her, she thought tidily and made her way to the shower.

"It was your idea in the first place."

"My idea?" Maggie's face was shocked, incredulous. The utter betrayal of history.

"Yes. You know damn well it was your idea. I'm one that's out of a goddamn nineteen thirty-eight black and white. Non-monogamy didn't exist then. Anyway, it's just a fancy word for adultery." BJ was excited and when she was excited Maggie was alive.

"I guess it all depends on your point of view." Maggie was aware the others had all arrived and she and BJ were still airing their dirty laundry. "Besides, that isn't even what we were arguing about. I don't care how breeders respond to romance. I'm talking about being out to the whole goddamn universe and how other people respond to that is their responsibility. Not mine."

BJ shook her head and added a there's-no-use-trying roll of her eyes to deflect Maggie's ire.

Tara, Lynn and Adrienne stood awkwardly, waiting like school children for their seat assignments.

"Well sit," Maggie barked. She waited until they found their individual spots, shook off her anger and motioned Noel to join her by the fireplace.

"That's always been your problem, Maggs." BJ's voice had a tone of finality to it: this conversation is closed, but I'm going to get the last word in. "You're trying to educate the universe. You know, some people just aren't interested."

"I don't give a good shit if they're interested or not. We're here and they're going to have to deal with us."

"So shove it down their throats, right?"

Noel put a hand to Maggie's elbow to calm her and make peace. "Another friendly debate, girls?"

Maggie stopped to consider how bent out of shape she could get if she wanted to. "Yeah...yeah." She let it drop. "Anyone make coffee?"

Tara jumped in with both feet. "Lynn took care of it for us. Such a shinin' domestic."

"Domesticity is sorely underappreciated in today's culture. The most fundamental task sheds light on primal survival...healing in its pure simplicity." The words floated out of Shilo, cloaked in a mysterious air of unreality as if her communication were programed from another planet.

"Of course, uh...darlin'," Tara replied, uncertainly. "It's just... I'm so hopelessly impaired."

Maggie leaned to Noel and breathed into her neck, "Must have been all that slavery."

"When my mother sent me to finishin' school, they took one look at me and simply knew I was hopeless. My intellect has always been my greatest asset, but it just flies right out the winda when it finds itself in the kitchen."

"We all have different talents," Shilo intoned. "That's what maintains harmonious balance."

Maggie could barely contain herself as she whispered

to Noel again, "Jesus Christ...it's Nirvana-go-Lucky from Crystal Mountain." Noel stifled a chuckle as Maggie interjected some order. "OK girls...This is the part where we go around, tell each other about our little lives...and get the dish."

****

"No, no, no, don't tell me." The deep, pleasant, almost melodious voice belongs to a tall, dark-haired stranger. His GQ attire and smoldering sensuality are in stark contrast to Humpwhale Inn's coastal setting. Claire is equally out of place. She is overdressed in a black cocktail dress, hair swept back into a French knot. She does not look directly at him, but through the mirror behind the bar as she lights a cigarette.

"I wouldn't dream of it."

"Scorpio." His sensitive eyes sparkle as he and Claire continue their repartee. When Claire smiles it's like fireworks. "Astrology's so..."

"...cosmic." They're both flip.

"Isn't it though." He takes a smooth sip of whiskey. "Isn't this the part where you're supposed to guess what I am?"

"Oh, but I know what you are."

"'It's the two-step of communication. One forward, one back, until any progress made is forgotten. Innuendo muddies the water.'" BJ read from her book, *The History of Communication*. "'Eskimos have three hundred words that indicate snow. And though we think of English as a complex language, there is a great need for more words to accurately accommodate subtlety, nuance—'"

****

He lights her cigarette. She deftly cups his hand. Her blue eyes catch the gleam from his lighter, royal blue aflame as she smiles, white teeth flashing, her lashes even smiling in invitation. She's been here a thousand times and when his eyes answer back she knows just how she will turn her head, just how she will angle her neck, so. Coy. The effect works. She can see he's hooked.

He considers, changes tactics. "You're not from around here." *Claire barely nods as if his observation is hardly worthy of note.* "And you're not going to make this easy are you?" *He waits.* "I guess not." *His face softens, his eyes are genuine.* "It's been a while since I engaged in...uh, verbal tango. And you may have noticed I don't exactly fit into the fisherman's motif."

"You didn't strike me as local color."

"See how much we have in common?"

"What would bring a nice cosmopolitan boy like yourself to the rural northwest?"

"I'm an investment broker...I'm actually tying up a rather hefty real estate deal—"

"Ahhh, raping the land—"

"— for a non-profit health care facility."

Claire salutes his efforts as she is taken down a peg.

Brian watches her readjust. "Let me guess," *he muses.* "A high-powered executive with a chip on her shoulder...tired of playing games." *Claire's eyes tell him he's guessed wrong.* "A runaway heiress. No. Too Frank Capra." *He peers into her eyes.* "But you are hiding. From something. Running, maybe. Getting over a rotten love affair."

Claire laughs. "And an imagination."

"Well, it keeps things interesting."

"Yes." *Claire assesses him as she takes a seductive drag off her cigarette.* "I bet it does."

****

"Well." Lynn was shy but eager. "I've been playing around with this idea for a long time. I mean I'm only a housewife...I'm usually so busy...I've only had time for an outline. I hope to get a first draft done while I'm here—while the twins are out of my hair." Lynn flustered her hands about in her lap. "Anyway, it's about this planet where men have to go through childbirth in order to be eligible for what I call the alpha society."

There was a sort of stunned silence. Lynn watched them expectantly.

"Why   darlin'...how,   uh,   innovative."   Tara condescendingly patted her on the knee as she picked up a fat flowery-jacketed novel.

Before anyone could say a word, she opened to a pre-marked page and took a deep breath of anticipation. "'The heat. Unbearably scorching as his strong, masculine, but gentle fingers touched her dainty hand. Alexandria could not deny the flutterin' beneath her swelling breasts, for she knew in an instant this handsome stranger could never be an evil traitor at all, but a kind man, of noble birth.'" Tara swallowed, swept away by her own words. "'Derrick Rochester's slate-gray eyes bored burnin' questions through the shock of pitch-black hair that fell over his forehead, givin' him the appearance of a darin' pirate. And then she saw his throbbin' manliness, visible as his lean muscular thighs neared her tremblin' presence. He held out his hand. The waltz was beginnin'. Dare she dance this dance of forbidden love?'"

****

Their legs are entwined, slithering to the music. They dance well together. Smooth, liquid. A subtle bump and grind. He holds her close, dips her slightly. Their eyes meet. She teases him, glances away.

Another bar. Another time. The cowboy. She loved cowboys. They were so uncomplicated. They treated you like a queen and were so unstudied in bed. They just did what came naturally. And they smelled of sweet hay, Jack Daniels and sweat.

It had been a gala celebrity-hosted party where none of the celebrities showed up. Just their names. All of them were the same. Ex-celebrities honoring the nouveau chic. Claire was one of them. Her second novel was already number three and climbing.

He was coming her way. Definite swagger. She liked that; confidence. He walked up to her, tilted his hat, ever so charming. She wanted to say "Let's fuck" and cut to the chase, but knew better. He'd prefer a 'lil lady-like maneuvering. Was it worth it? Claire was restless.

"You're the writer."

"You're the cowboy."

He smiled, underneath a beautiful trimmed Hershey chocolate moustache. His eyes were Reese's brown to match. Yes she could eat him right up.

"You write those women's books, don't ya?"

"What do you do?"

"I'm a stunt man."

"Dangerous."

"Excitin'."

"You enjoy being on the edge." It was a statement. Claire learned early on statements were always much more provocative than questions.

"I like my work, if that's what you mean."

Her voice was soft and silky, a soothing trickle from a fountain. "I'd like to hear all about your work."

Later he lit a cigarette, pulled himself up against the double pillows, offered it to her.

"Ain't you a surprise?"

She cocked her brow as she accepted the cigarette.

"Most wimmin like you, all so cool-like, so untouchable sorta, ain't exactly a wild bronco ride, if ya catch my drift."

"I think I catch it." She inhaled deeply. When she exhaled her sigh was deep. And her eyes, empty.

****

"Words. Float. Meaningless." Adrienne's tone mimicked an Obsession commercial. "Labels-separate. Language-binds. But if there is none?"

They waited. It appeared the poem was over. Lynn was shell-shocked. "That's so..."

"Spiritual," Shilo supplied as Adrienne came out of her trance.

"Personally I think we should create a Woman-Language dictionary to incorporate all the nuances we have no verbiage for—"

"Oh shit!" Maggie cut Adrienne off. "I can see it now. Men pulling out pocketbook translators, stashed right behind the Copenhagen."

"Oh, don't be such a goddamn separatist." BJ was familiarly annoyed. "Men are just as invested in clearer communication as we are."

"Then why do we have such a goddamn time understanding one another?"

"Because we communicate in two different languages." Everyone turned to Noel who had spoken for the first time.

"So they're different. The only thing important is the language of loving..." Shilo became mystical as BJ rolled her eyes. "...the universal dance, the 'primal' connection."

"Ya'll talkin' about the evil deed?"

Maggie deflected Tara. "No, she's talkin' about the great debate."

"Well, as far as I'm concerned that's all the language we need," she said in fiery persistence.

Maggie saw the claws and thought with renewed interest: perhaps there lurked the spirit of a rebel underneath Tara's ample bosom. "That's exactly what the cavewoman said after she was raped, I bet."

"Maggie!!"

"Yeah, yeah." Maggie gulped her beer. "Shilo, your turn." Shilo didn't respond. "Earth to Shilo... You know, what you're working on."

"Oh...oh yes." Shilo rejoined their frequency. "An herbal cookbook with an emphasis on chakra nutrients to heal inner-child deficiencies which can not be accessed through re-birthing."

"Oh—Kay." Even Maggie found herself at a loss for words. "You heard it here, folks."

"And what about Dr. Benedict?" Tara needled, "Ya'll wrote *The Naked Truth.* Stirred up quite a hornet's nest."

"Noel's like that." Maggie's voice was full of admiration.

"Tell me, Dahk-tah. Don't you think some things are better left unsaid?"

"Yes," Noel agreed. "And I've noticed how well you've adhered to that economy of expression in...what was it?"

"*Lust in the Night,*" Maggie answered for Tara. Tara was noticeably rebuffed as Noel nonchalantly sipped her tea.

****

Her back glistens in the glow of the motel sign as she rides his muscular form below her. She falls forward. Her breath is ragged, raspy. Her eyes are closed. When she opens them there is a sadness in them. Before the emptiness can fill them up, she leans back. She slides forward as she extricates herself from him, takes a pack of cigarettes from the night stand. She lights up, passes the cigarette to him and exhales. He takes it, tries to touch her face gently, but she moves before he can make contact. She takes the cigarette back and then hides behind a smile. Practiced. So practiced even she barely knows it's not real.

The sounds of desperate search echoed from the bathroom. Noel shifted on the couch trying to refocus on the report she was reading but the noises continued and grew louder as Claire rummaged through the contents of the hutch, opening and closing each and every drawer with entirely too much emphasis. Noel watched her, irritation mounting, holding the report futilely in one hand as Claire's hunt resumed in the kitchenette. Noel's nerves finally gave out

"Can I help you with something?"

"Aspirin."

Noel got up. Moments later she returned with a bottle, holding it out to Claire with condescension. "Rough night?"

"No pain," Claire shrugged, "no gain."

"There might be an easier way." Noel returned to her

seat as Claire gingerly slouched into the chair opposite her.

"You would know, right? That's what you do isn't it? Tinker with fucked up psyches."

"Hardly a term I'd apply to my practice." Noel pretended to read the dry, endless text.

Claire shifted. She attempted to find a position that would remotely make her feel like being inside her skin again, but as the pain behind her eyes continued to twist like burnt pokers in the back of her brain she gave up. She decided to try and make Noel miserable as well. "Let's just say I've never met a shrink who was any less fucked up than the people they are trying to fix."

"We're only human."

"If a surgeon was missing a big piece of themselves, like say a hand, or an eye, I'd expect him or *her* to find another profession."

"We're all missing pieces. It doesn't mean we can't help someone else find theirs."

Claire chugged some water, throwing back her head as she gulped the aspirin. She tossed the bottle onto the couch near Noel. "You therapists are so good at handing out aspirin...and the obvious."

"Well, if it were so obvious, I doubt you'd be struggling so successfully."

Noel walked from the cabin, leaving Claire's swollen head to digest this as well as could be expected at such an ungodly hour of the morning.

****

"I want another room!" Noel grabbed the book from Maggie's lap.

"What?"

"I'm not in the mood for experimental cohabitation."

"N-o-o—e-el." Maggie tried to cajole Noel who paced angrily in front of her.

"I can't get any work done. She's intrusive with her running in all hours of the night. She's...she's a slut. A common garden variety slut!"

"Don't you think that's a little harsh?" BJ strolled in from the dining room.

"Harsh...I don't think there's a more appropriate term."

"I don't know. She sounds a bit like one of your archetype heroines." BJ sat next to Maggie.

"What?"

BJ feigned the affected intellectual. "Hmmmm let me see. Something about loose women being the champions of non-monogamy." BJ picked up a copy of Noel's *The Naked Truth*. "And I quote, '...a more realistic approach to long term relationships than the repeatedly unsuccessful exclusivity set up by marriage, which results in serial monogamy as opposed to long-term coupling.'"

"Yeah, Dr. Benedict," Maggie interjected. "I'd think you'd want to study this specimen up close."

"She hardly belongs in that category." Noel clamped her jaws shut. "Is there another room?"

"You know there isn't."

Noel dropped Maggie's book back in her lap. "Perhaps I should consider my options."

"Yes, Noel," BJ countered, but not unkindly, "perhaps you should."

****

She had only seen her father cry once, shortly before her seventeenth birthday, on the tenth anniversary of her mother's death. The bus had broken down on its way home from school. Her father's panic had escalated and when she finally arrived, he grasped her to him savagely, his British upbringing in tattered shreds as he clutched his offspring in primal protection. It was only then that she realized there was a place in her father's heart reserved for a fiercely intense love that belonged to her, and only her.

When her mother had died so had the warmth in her father's eyes. For several years she was fostered by her father's sister, Aunt Sheila, whose voice reminded her of frozen icicles. She became a prisoner of good breeding and Aunt Sheila's inborn resentment of her own facile upbringing and therefore her greatest quest in life: to instill her own prim manners and upper girl's school etiquette upon Noel. But Noel consistently disappointed her aunt. She kept to herself, reading for long hours into the night and when she did say anything it was insufferably tactless. She went out of her way to speak her mind, even if she did so quietly. Aunt Sheila believed her anti-social behavior was Noel's mastermind plan to drive her to the ultimate disgrace: losing her temper. The child had to be taught the difference between unmindful honesty and gracious diplomacy. And the more withdrawn Noel became, the more arch and insistent Aunt Sheila's stiff-upper-lip demands became. After all, she and Charles had gone out of their way to help her poor, bereft younger brother, who had had no sense marrying Noel's mother in the first place, bloody American singer who was as wild as the night was black. And her offspring—genetic twist, that. She couldn't have looked any more like her mother. Poor David. It would certainly be a hardship to have his wife's mirror image before him. But she couldn't tolerate the child's utter lack of social finesse. Her manners were deplorable.

Finally, wearing the weary look of someone who has been tested beyond her mettle, Aunt Sheila returned his daughter to her brother, and told him, with what she considered quite respectable melodrama, that the child simply was not normal.

David Benedict was just as much at a loss in raising his daughter as his sister had been. He and Noel kept to themselves, passing each day as silently as the last. When they did talk it was to discuss when he would next be leaving for business and how long he would be gone. Did she need anything. New clothes, items for school. It was not that he was unkind. He was simply not present.

Noel was aware of a vast emptiness, but had no idea how to fill it. She preoccupied herself with her schooling and the world she created every time she turned the page of a new book. Her life was as exciting as Hemingway's adventures, as droll and sublime as Wilde's affairs, as sarcastic as Parker's cynical poems, and as richly textured as Ayn Rand's cornerstone tomes. But it was all in her head and only occasionally did any of it travel to her heart.

It was because of this naturally cultivated detachment that Noel found herself exceedingly gifted in helping others resolve emotional problems by remaining objective in the face of the most tortured anguish. And in doing so Noel was able to experience the gift of healing which was as close as she was able to come in divining a sense of spirituality. If her emotional bedside manner left something to be desired, her clients sought her directive intellectual approach and left more fully evolved, balanced and healthy. She was, by any standard, a success. Her practice thrived, she was extremely well thought of in the women's health care field, respectably notorious with the male practitioners, and her patients adored her. But the hole was still a hole.

She had stormed from Maggie's cabin with the same sense of futility she had often felt when she was trapped with her Aunt Sheila—firmly aware of the gnawing emptiness with no idea how to fill it. She headed to the beach. She had so much work to do and here she was, stomping around in the sand like a child, frustrated, trying to remember everything she was about. Calmness. Serenity. Collecting the data and then assessing a situation without jumping to conclusions. What was the bottom line? What was bothering her so about this intrusive personality? She had worked with difficult people before and remained utterly untouched. How could she fix it? Fixing it was, after all, what she was supposed to be so damn good at.

A large rock loomed, seemingly out of nowhere. Her gait slowed. She studied the monolith, advancing curiously to explore the craggy exterior. Her hand followed the jutting history of a million years, then she slowly turned in to it and pressed the full length of her body against its granite strength. She closed her eyes and let the sun beat on her back, hoping it would penetrate this sense of defeat she hadn't felt in years. She squared her shoulders and slowly headed back to the cabin.

****

Noel was relieved Claire wasn't parked in the front room. It was easier if she had a moment to think before she approached her. She paced quietly, structuring her thoughts and sentences so there would be no room for misunderstanding, priding herself on her gift for clarity of communication. When she felt prepared she trod lightly towards Claire's room, knocked gently on the door. There was no answer. But Noel could sense Claire's presence on the other side. She knocked again.

"Yeah?" Distant, remote.

"Can I interrupt you a moment?" There was a silence, and Noel was sure she heard a sigh of discontent.

"Yeah."

Noel opened the door. As usual, the tendrils of smoke from Claire's cigarette floated towards her. Claire sat in the middle of her bed Indian-style amidst clutter and mayhem as she stared at her laptop. Clothes, cassettes, papers, files, and an inordinate number of books, opened and carelessly strewn about, were piled everywhere, so that Noel wondered if Claire removed the debris every night before she retired only to spend the next day rebuilding it.

Claire was clearly not in the mood for conversation and barely glanced Noel's way, but Noel was intent upon her mission. "Do you suppose we might arrive at an understanding?"

Claire observed her cigarette as if it were the most intriguing artifact she had ever encountered, and then without further ado, mashed it into an ashtray suffocated by butts. "I doubt it."

"A compromise."

"Look. We're just polar opposites. No biggie. You stay north and I'll stay south."

Noel paused before she replied. "Then perhaps some ground rules to help smooth things out."

"Rules," Claire smirked. "You shrinks just love them, don't you. 'Be spontaneous. Love life. Embrace it. But do it by the rules.'"

"Are you finished?" Claire did not answer. "I came here to work. But it is extremely difficult to be...this fragmented. I would like for this situation to be bearable for both of us."

Claire turned to her, relenting slightly. "Yeah."

"Good. First of all our schedules are radically different. Your hours are diametrically opposed to my own. In order for us to mesh into some sort of routine, I suggest we arrange for certain hours we each use the bathroom, kitchen, and common areas. Furthermore..."

But Claire didn't hear the rest of Noel's assessment of the situation. It wasn't that she didn't want it to be workable. It was simply that whenever rules and ultimatums were thrown in her face, she went into a state of autism. She pretended to follow, but instead her mind wandered, and Noel's words faded in futile assaults against the void.

****

Two nights later, Claire strolled in, a little more than tipsy, knocking into the hutch. One of the Wedgwood cups teetered precariously before Claire caught it. God knew, the British Empire might collapse if Noel didn't have her favorite teacup in the morning. She noticed the light from beneath Noel's door. She was still at work. God, the woman never stopped. Claire spent a moment wondering whether she admired Noel's discipline or despaired over it, then tried to remember what the rule was about showering times. Shit. She should have paid more attention, but really. This woman's obsession with order was beyond the pale. Claire decided best not to get caught up in it. She would simply stay out of the way. Hell, she spent most of her nights out anyway. Besides, rules were for people who were afraid of themselves. Certainly not anarchists like herself.

Noel heard the movements from the other room. God, did the woman never stay home? How could she ever get anything accomplished when she spent half her time in bars? Noel stared at the screen of her laptop. Oh, God. Claire was taking another shower. The bathroom would be a complete mess in the morning. Noel stretched her neck, rubbed the tough knot forming in her right shoulder. A fleeting thought of envy flashed through her mind, and then was just as quickly squelched. The idea of that kind of wild freedom was nothing but frightening.

Bullshit!" BJ was particularly feisty this evening and Maggie was certain it was due to cunnilingus interruptus. Just as they had started making love, Lynn had pounded on the door, a half hour early for Tuesday evening's festivities. The three of them sat, filling the void with unusually inane conversation, the crackling fire punctuating the heat generated more by BJ's desire than the blazing logs. Finally the rest of the group arrived, seating themselves informally on the couch and floor in a semi-circle as the fire continued to roar.

Lynn stared at BJ, open-mouthed, as she had most of the evening as BJ said, "If anything our complacency has made us take two steps backwards."

"It's the same ol' thing." Adrienne sighed. "If they keep telling us how far you've come baby we believe it."

"And our boys will keep jumping into the arena." BJ's eyes were aflame. "Blood-thirsty gladiators wielding car phones, drunk with espresso and martini brunches—"

"Real men don't brunch—" quipped Maggie.

"— intoxicated by their power," Adrienne concluded.

"But..." Lynn interjected an opinion. "...But we have made a lot of advances."

"Certainly we have, sugah." Tara patted her on the knee.

"Yeah 'sugah,'" Adrienne quipped. "Haven't you heard of Nutrasweet?"

Lynn's eyes darted frantically, like those of a child who is trying to comprehend the logic of its elders. "Well...what I mean is...I mean all you have to do is look at history. We vote. We work and still have children. We're a lot better off than we were...and we do have equal footing."

"Mass control." BJ yawned affectedly.

"I mean if you just realize what women do today." Lynn's earnestness grew with each word. "Carpenters! Women who run their own businesses...Airline pilots...the accomplishments! There's a lot less discrimination. We're better paid and we hold jobs of...of distinction."

"Yeah." Maggie lit a cigarette. "As ball busters." At the pained expression on Lynn's face Maggie added sweetly, "Darlin' you've eaten every last bite the media has spoon-fed ya, like a good little girl."

"I think women who value their femininity can maintain it if they just play the game right." Tara reached for her wine.

"Sure, if they want to be passive-aggressive." Adrienne needled her.

"And remember," BJ warned, "we're not granted that all-powerful trait men uphold as a birthright. Arrogance."

"Ooooohhhh yeah." Adrienne jumped up, her long limbs flailing excitedly. "I'd love to be a man. Waltz into a room, scope out what I want like I'm looking over apples at the fruit stand. If I did that I'd be a—"

"— slut." Claire supplied with a cynical edge.

So the ice-goddess speaks. Maggie watched them all study Claire, who stared, motionless, at the floor.

"Exactly! But a man, he simply adjusts his balls." Adrienne mocked this motion. "Goes in swinging."

"But when a woman goes in swinging, it's a come-on." Again there was a sharp twist to Claire's voice, as if the knowledge was hard-earned. "She's a tart. A nasty girl. A bitch."

"What do you think, Noel?" Maggie prodded. If she could get things stirred up, tonight just might turn out to be interesting.

Noel seemed to choose her words carefully. "I think the double standard remains firmly intact. Especially with women."

"What?" Lynn was astounded.

"Have you forgotten about the women's movement?" Tara baited.

"Not at all." Noel was matter-of-fact. "But we've been apologizing for it ever since. Like a child discovering its independence. It crawls bravely out, but once poised upon the precipice of danger, it scurries back to its mother. We don't allow anyone, or certainly ourselves, any power, let alone individuality."

"You mean...sexual preference?" Tara pushed.

"All of it. Theoretically we're an evolved group of women." Noel encompassed them all. "Who for one reason or another find judgment with one another's lifestyles, work, compromises—"

"Some compromises..." Tara pointed her remark at Noel, "just aren't worth it."

"If by that you're implying my lesbianism—"

Lynn's head swiveled to Noel as Tara deported her body in a self-servingly smug manner. Claire's eyes sparked with interest at this new information and she observed Noel carefully.

"If I had chosen any other way, it would have been the most costly compromise I could make. But you have illustrated my point. You're appalled by my choices." The battle line was clearly drawn between Noel and Tara. "I don't take it personally. Even lesbians don't allow for much diversity within our subculture. We're simply still too afraid to take our power."

"Maybe collectively." Again they turned to the unexpected source of this comment. Noel appeared surprised Claire would have anything to add. Maggie watched intently. "But individually there is an enormous power in being female. If you know how to use it."

"Exactly." Tara obviously felt supported. The ranks were choosing sides.

"And I'm not talkin' lash-battin' feminine wiles." Claire cut Tara with her southern drawl. "I mean taking their rules and shoving it up their asses."

"All right!" Adrienne was thrilled.

"The best part being," Claire continued mischievously, "they don't have a clue they're being butt-fucked."

A silence hit the room. Lynn looked as if she had been struck with a switch. Such foul language and from a lady, no less. Tara's fine breeding asserted itself as she haughtily attempted to compose herself.

"Where's the power in that game?" Noel countered.

"It's no game, I assure you." Claire rose, tired of the debate.

"Then where is the joy?"

Claire sauntered towards Noel, stopped just short of a foot from her. "Joy?" Claire's tone was flip, but her eyes were deadly serious. "I'm talking about survival."

****

Claire smoked her cigarette outside. What a fool! She

considered herself sophisticated, aware. So why did Noel's exposing her sexuality affect her so? Of course, she had known it all along. Claire took a deeper drag than she intended. The smoke hurt her lungs. She just hadn't voiced it to herself. God. What was she doing here? These women! A bunch of drippy unenlightened neophytes pretending at worldly conversation. She would have been better off passing the evening away at that abysmal excuse for a bar.

Claire threw her cigarette butt to the ground, swirled the dregs of her wine on top of it. As she returned to the kitchen she stopped. She heard Tara, Lynn and Adrienne washing the remainder of the cups and wine glasses.

"I don't know," Tara pouted, "it just sorta gives me the willies. I mean I'm as open-minded as the next person, but there's something...I don't know, unnatural about it all."

"But she looks as normal as you or I." There was a hint of desperation in Lynn's voice. If Noel could be the woman next door, she could be her as well. Poor thing, thought Claire. Housewife dementia. She heard the strain Lynn's mind was taking into uncharted territory.

"All I can say, is what a waste!"

"Why Missy O'Hara." Adrienne affected a southern twang. "For such an open-minded soul, you sure are talkin' like an ignorant misguided bigot." Claire peeked in just far enough to see Adrienne playfully fling a dishtowel at Tara, who turned away, looking unsure as to whether she wanted to let the slam go or not. Adrienne's eyes were playful, teasing. Tara gave the best southern-forgiven pout she could muster in return.

"She's very attractive." Lynn was still pondering. "I guess I don't understand. Maybe she was abused or—"

"Boy you are from the burbs, aren't you." Adrienne was condescending.

"Personally, I think it's a defect of nature," Tara pronounced with finality.

Claire could endure no more. She brought in her wine glass, set it down with emphasis and turned to her. "Well. Who would better know about defects than a southerner, Miz Tara."

Claire made her exit leaving them in utter silence.

****

Claire walked in the moonlight back to the cabin. She couldn't get it off her mind. Lesbian. Letting the word float through her mind, the ramifications digging somewhere beyond her subconscious, she almost tripped over a large stump.

She let herself into the cabin and stood in the middle of the dark living room. Noel was still at Maggie's. She knew she shouldn't but something about the woman, the tall handsome woman's containment of her own essence drove Claire to a curiosity to understand something, anything about her. Her being a...a lesbian.

She crept towards Noel's room.

It was very much as she expected. Contained. Everything in its place. Orderly. Claire stopped when she saw the beautiful artwork adorning the walls, orchestrated around one full-length oil painting of a nude female whose arched back and muscular movement made it feasible the form might storm from the canvas. She found herself propelled towards it.

She studied it for several moments and then gingerly, apprehensively put her hand to the lines of the woman's neck, tracing the sinewy musculature to the edge of her breast.

The painting made her think of two young girls, both thirteen, at a private slumber party. She and her best friend, Janet, in their full-length cotton nightgowns, scrubbed clean and pretty. They laughed and played, teasing each other, until Claire's hand had reached over and something about the way she touched Janet's forearm made them both stop. They had become very serious as Claire followed the line of her arm up to the soft cottony envelope of Janet's very young breast. Claire remembered that later, as she lay very still next to Janet, Janet's breathing had been as shallow as her own, and neither of them had slept a wink.

"She was a client."

Claire jumped back from the painting and her ancient memory. She was so off-guard that she could not turn to face the woman whose room she had just invaded.

"We enjoyed the best of the barter system."

"They're good." Claire continued to stare at the painting, composing herself. "Strong. Energetic." She finally turned. "I didn't mean to intrude. I was just..."

"Wondering?" Noel smiled.

Claire returned the smile briefly with her eyes.

"I'm beginning to think you're right about those meetings." Noel sighed as if with an old frustration.

"Women can't help themselves. Latent bitchiness. Must be in the Y chromosome."

There was an awkward silence. Claire felt she should leave. She took a chance and looked at the handsome woman studying the painting. As usual, she was dressed in a smart blazer, navy blue with an angora cream turtleneck sweater underneath. Claire wanted to touch the soft material. She cleared her throat. "You know we're outnumbered."

"Hmmmm?"

"Well, I don't know if you've noticed it, but we are surrounded by dangerously bizarre women."

They both laughed. Claire knew she should leave, but somehow couldn't. "How about a nightcap?"

As Noel considered the offer Claire found herself desperately wanting this woman who had annoyed her so much to accept the invitation.

"Scotch OK?" Claire felt shy.
"Scotch is particularly OK."

****

Claire rummaged about in the hutch as Noel built a fire. Maggie's own proclivities to drink made her generous in the stocking of beverages. Claire pulled out an unopened bottle of Chivas Regal, her father's favorite, and joined Noel who had made herself comfortable on the pillows in front of the hearth. Claire sat, poured them both a drink. They toasted silently.

"I'd say you've got balls, but you'd probably take it wrong."

"What?" Noel was confused.

"Tonight. Being so..." Claire searched. "Out."

"Oh, that. Well, it would hardly do my readers or patients any good if I cowered behind protocol." Noel took a contemplative sip of her scotch. A light rain began to fall. Claire huddled closely to herself as she began to warm by the fire. She watched Noel's profile in the flickering shadows and thought what a uniquely handsome woman she was. Androgynous. Her chiseled features made her appear stern as she stared into the fire, but when she turned and looked directly into Claire's eyes, the openness in her eyes softened her visage.

"It isn't a problem is it?" Noel's voice was careful, tentative.

"Not for me."

"Some women...they—"

"Don't worry. I have no inner homophobia... that's what you shrinks call it right? Inner homophobia?" Claire teased good-naturedly, and showed Noel a side of her that few seldom got to see—the genuine, when she didn't feel the need to be acerbic or biting. Claire felt suddenly exposed.

She turned her attention to the fire and felt her edge return as she posited in a more serious tone, "I'm into whatever feels good for the moment."

"And after that?" Noel countered.

Claire took a slow swallow of her drink. "I wait for the next moment."

A lazy gull floated nonchalantly above the crashing waves then darted in, flirting with danger. Claire scouted its motion as she stood on the precipice of a jutting rock overlooking the coastline, at the end of a small rocky path that wrapped around either side of the recessed beach. She stared at the waves, entranced by their volatile motion, then glanced to her left—the south—watching the tide rush over the sand, and thought about further south. The city.

A city full of swarming egos and inexhaustible friendliness. A city where celebrities banded together to save the planet from extinction but in their hectic schedules left their basic human values behind in the last meeting they took. A town filled with stereotypes and caricatures. You couldn't aspire to a more redundant equation, except television already had. A town without trust.

And speaking of trust, there were the men. Plenty

of men. Her first experience at seventeen. No one ever
believed she had remained a virgin until she was seventeen
so she stopped discussing it altogether. It even amazed
her now. But escaping her mother and Jake at the age of
fourteen, she spent every hour of life simply trying to
survive: waitressing, electrical assembly work, telephone
solicitation—any number of equally reputable experiences
all pockmarked her resume as she wrote it all down in the
nights, endlessly, repetitively, redundantly, spewing out
her experience, reliving every ugly nightmare until she
had exorcised the worst of it.

During those late night hours she discovered the
merits of drink to ease the pressures of the day. At first
all she could afford was rotgut wine and cheap Potters
Bourbon while she scribbled long and furious, instilling an
illusory sense of inspiration with each passing glass. She
was not inordinately fond of liquor but somewhere along
the line she had grown attached to a romantic ideal of the
disheveled writer and her bottle; presenting the image of
herself in her younger, more idealistic years as a latter day
female Hemingway, adopting his live-hard, play-hard lust
for life. Then when her life became a different breed of
playground full of cynical and cutthroat playmates and
her sexual dance card became a roulette game of chance,
she had found that the best way to absorb it all was to blur
the edges of reality with a drink or two, making fun of it
and herself.

After years of rejection, her first manuscript, a cynical
novel mimicking *The Catcher in the Rye* as seen through
female eyes, became a national best seller. Critics
called it "a hot, sexy page turner." She had filled it with
foul language between a young man and woman who
couldn't decide whether they wanted to get married or
live in blissful sin, all the while surrounding themselves
with sexual playmates until the heroine or antagonist,

depending on one's point of view, became pregnant. The advance had more than paid the bills. The book's success snagged a hefty option for a TV movie, and resulted in her acquiring a snarly agent who'd cut up studio suits for hors d'oeuvres, gnaw on them over dinner meetings, and spit them out the next time they "did lunch." This paved the way for her second and third books which had led to the overwhelming success of *Life Can Ruin Your Hair* which made her a sort of Gloria Steinem of the unpolitical eighties "gimme" set who approached life without any regard for ramification. Now she could live comfortably, she had achieved recognition, she was well-thought-of in most circles even if sarcasm got the best of her when she drank a bit too much.

Claire had never been what she would term "sexually promiscuous," until *Life* stormed the nation. She spent too many nights in empty hotel rooms on tour and too little time attempting what she had become terrified to even contemplate: writing. Really writing. A novel that made a difference. She suspected that her talent was wasted, if she indeed ever had any, and after a time she decided that spending endless hours agonizing over it was an additional squander of time. Instead, she would go to the hotel's bar, to sample the "local color." She met an enormous variety of men and experienced the spectrum of wonderful and not so wonderful lovers.

"Wonderful" was a term she tossed about casually when she gauged her lovers. There was awful, bad, OK and then those rare specimens who were actually considerate and concerned with her pleasure as well as their own. There were even a few who were "wonderful" conversationalists but horrific listeners. When it first occurred to her that sexual exploits were at best utterly inconsequential, the realization shook her very foundation. She had grinned weakly, remembering Woody Allen's proverb that there was no such thing as "a bad orgasm." But she was fairly certain the physical sensation all the storybooks were alluding to, what the old standards had crooned about for decades, and even today's drippy ballads screeched at anyone who cared to listen at ear-shattering decibels, was not what she was experiencing. And it was in that private moment when she knew something was missing and terribly wrong.

But she kept the seed of that knowledge firmly cloaked in darkness. And on the rare occasions she let it see the light of day, she became so frightened by the emptiness of her life that she immediately tucked it back into the recesses of her subconscious. She began to take great pride in her absolute autonomy and to contend that her male escorts were merely a means to an end.

But there was a new emptiness she had only recently recognized and one she could not gloss over. And the nagging question she asked herself more often than not these days: Now what? She shook her head, not willing to think of it. A modern day Scarlett O'Hara. *I'm dealing with it*, one part of her argued. The other simply looked north.

About a mile out a large rock caught her fascination and before she knew what had compelled her, she found herself heading towards it.

****

If she were to describe this place she would call it a magical forest in a childhood fairyland, so removed from her real life was this sanctuary of dark and forbidden forest. She had been following the rough path down the ravine of overgrown blackberry vines, when it appeared—the mysterious and enchanting isle of somber shadows, quiet stillness, where she came to sit for long periods, in contemplation, or writing. The only light that streamed through the towering evergreens and overgrown fern life reflected off her gold pen as she now dashed several lines in her journal.

I don't know why I remembered this about Erika, but she hated grapes. That big fruit bowl they gifted at the hotel, she wouldn't touch them. She ate everything around them, the kiwi, bananas, oranges, fed me strawberries so sweetly.

They had spent a glorious weekend at the Columbia Gorge Hotel "nestled romantically in the gently wooded forests with a spectacular view of the river" or so the pamphlet had promised. It wouldn't have mattered if they were in a dungeon, Noel thought at the time. They had ordered room service and made love the entire weekend, laughed, talked and giggled, and the few moments they did stare out the window, the heaving river was indeed spectacular. But Noel only had eyes for Erika's profile, the sweet tilt of her head, those brown eyes that brimmed with tears, so full of surprise and wonder every time Noel made love to her, as if she had given her the most incredible gift in the world. And each time Erika would hold her closer. And, finally, at the end she sobbed, anguished moans as Noel held her protectively and told her there was nothing to worry about. Erika insisted Noel didn't understand, couldn't understand about her life, the insanity of her situation.

Noel stroked her face calmly. "We'll work on it together."

"Yes." Erika had replied weakly.

"That's all that matters." Noel tried to buoy her strength.

Erika grasped her frantically. "Promise."

"Promise."

"No matter what."

"Erika."

Now I remember. It was Claire. She was eating grapes at Maggie's the other night, and then again this morning. But she doesn't exactly eat them. It's more like a savoring process, as if hunger had nothing at all to do with her eating of them...simply the way she enjoyed slicing them in half with her front teeth, then sucking the pulpy juice from them.

I suppose it could be quite sexy the way she eats them.

Oh, God! What am I doing here? Maybe this place no longer serves its purpose. There are simply too many memories. Why did I have to take my haven and introduce E. to it? Now, everywhere I turn, I see her and us last year. I can't get any work done. Of course, it doesn't help having the annoying Ms Jabrowski lurking in the shadows. And Maggie. I could wring her neck. She couldn't actually have thought Claire would take my mind off E?... OK, let's be fair. She has her moments. She can even be charming. Bottom line, I'm hoping she'll get fed up with the lack of pace and go back to LA where she belongs.

Noel sighed, closed the journal. She studied her surroundings without really taking them in. She emerged from the cavernous, wooded area and followed a path that overlooked Arcadia beach. She saw the rock out there. Her rock.

****

Claire approached the rock from one end and Noel from the opposite direction. As they both rounded the ocean boulder from either side, they discovered, simultaneously, a gaping rift that split it cleanly in two. There was a small path of sand, between, just wide enough to maneuver through.

They caught sight of each other in the same instant. For a moment, neither spoke. Claire slowly approached Noel, then stopped.

Noel felt foolish as she mumbled, "I...I was taking a break."

"It's not a crime." Claire smiled as she had the previous night, sincere. Her eyes were engaging as she moved forward.

Without words they began strolling companionably and silently along the tide.

After some time, Claire lit a cigarette. "She gets to you, doesn't she."

They both stopped then, sat on a rock. Claire prodded, "How can anyone like you take her seriously—"

"The Tara O'Haras of this world are the unwitting champions of patriarchy."

"Oh shit." Claire baited her playfully. "A PC Queen."

"Do I sound like I'm giving a lecture?" Noel grinned.

"Do you ever not?" Claire's eyes teased. She got up, touched Noel's arm, an invitation to follow her.

They walked for several hours, not saying much, simply sharing their isolation. Noel found herself feeling comfortable around Claire for the first time. Her edge had softened. There was something about Claire's quiet sincerity that engaged Noel, and she found herself enjoying Claire's curiosity and probing questions. At certain moments when she would catch Claire unaware there was an almost childlike eagerness in her face that belied the sarcastic cynicism and conveyed instead an untamed wild expectation that life was an experience to savor.

A monolith appeared around the bend in the coastline, set against a craggy backdrop whose edges had been softened by the constant lull of the incoming tides. It might have gone unnoticed but the golden sun cast a clay-rust hue to its exterior, throwing dramatic shadows behind the slender tapered form.

Noel walked around it several times. "It belongs in an art gallery."

Claire assessed its abstract form. "It's a woman."

"She's celebrating."

"What?" Claire walked around the other side of the form so that her face was just in the shadow. "What is she celebrating?"

"A million years of beauty." Noel indicated the rock's view.

"The keeper." Claire moved a step forward to touch the exterior and then to the side.

When the amber burnt sun caught Claire's face, Noel caught her breath. She clearly saw the ancient heritage, the firm jawline and wide-berthed cheekbones—a warrior, female Indian warrior, wild and tempestuous, ruled by primal need and desire.

Claire caught Noel studying her. "She's beautiful isn't she."

Noel kept her eyes steady on Claire. "Yes. She is."

****

"...and after that?"

"I studied in England. Oxford."

"So that's where the form over function comes in." Claire needled her, but gently. They were skirting the water's edge as they strolled, aimlessly.

"Perhaps."

"Why psychiatry?"

"I...I thought I'd be good at it."

"Are you?"

"I think so."

"What do your patients think?"

"Honestly?"

"Isn't that the first rule?"

"I think..." Noel paused and then walked forward. "I think my bedside manner leaves a little to be desired."

"Yes." Claire followed softly, "Mine as well."

****

The sun was lowering against the ocean in the late afternoon, painting the western sky with darkening blues, indigos and a brilliant crimson peach that lined the horizon.

"So...tell me about this pornography thing."

"It's an extension of a theory, actually."

"About—" Claire prodded.

"Our culture's struggle with intimacy. I mean we've so successfully sanitized sex—"

"Watch the alliteration."

"— there's nothing left to eroticize. The only time we can achieve a more potent sense of excitement is through taboo."

"Pornography being one act over the line from erotica."

"Close."

"And what's erotica?" Claire teased.

"You tell me."

"Well, you're the expert on this stuff." Claire pushed Noel playfully towards the water. "Aren't you, Doc?"

****

"What's one woman's poison?" Noel's fine-boned fingers played with the salt shaker in a small cafe. "Beauty is, after all, in the eyes of the beholder."

"Like *The Enchanted Cottage*."

"Yes. Great film." Noel entertained a deep interest in the salt shaker as she spoke. "I don't know if I've ever seen anything capture the concept better."

"Yes and in glorious black and white. Although you do have to give some credit to a film like *Edward Scissorhands*. It was after all saying the same thing."

"Give me an old black and white with a happy ending any day."

"Ahh..." Claire maneuvered the salt shaker from Noel's hand. Noel looked up. Claire's eyes danced lightly with hers. "A romantic."

"I find it remarkable—determining what moves someone." Noel recaptured the salt shaker to return to the safer side of the conversation.

"What moves you?"

The soft entreaty in Claire's voice threw Noel off track. Up until this point she had been fine with Claire's questions, but this was too private. To compose herself she assumed the role of Dr. Benedict, choosing her words cautiously. "Eroticism is a completely personal... individual...matter. Cultures, subcultures, are so uncomfortable with primal desires that we've gone to inordinate lengths to obliterate them. And, the medical community attempts to label everything, with this absurd Dewey Decimal System of never-ending and overlapping psychiatric diagnosis—"

"God, I thought that would appeal to your sense of order."

"You think I'm—"

"— anal," Claire finished for her. Noel laughed. "Do you enjoy it?"

Noel wasn't at all sure what she was referring to. "Enjoy what?"

"Your work."

Clair of The Moon 75

"Mostly." Noel cast about for explanation. "Sometimes I think it's a fantasy gone awry."

"But if—"

"— It's what this *romantic* does." A waitress arrived with their cappuccinos. "And you. You're a sarcastic contemporist."

"Is that a diagnosis?"

"No, it came from the jacket of your book, quote, view of the nineties—raw, real, racy."

"Then you've read it." There was a hesitation in Claire's voice.

"The jacket cover."

Claire was relieved. Somewhat.

"It claims you demystify the power struggle between the sexes while poking fun at the absurdity of the modern relationship."

"Yeah, well, it's like I said..." Claire returned to her sardonic tone.

"Yes, I know. You simply butt-fuck men right and left."

"That has nothing to do with my books." Claire burned her tongue as she sipped her cappuccino.

"A personal vendetta maybe." Noel's sense of professional detachment was lost and she couldn't stop herself.

"That's none of your business."

"Come on, Claire. You can dish it out—"

"Listen, Doc. Don't treat me like one of your patients."

Noel glanced at her hands, wondering why this woman had such effortless ability to pry beneath her skin. She begged for her containment to return, but as she caught the spark in Claire's fiery eyes and felt the tension flare between her shoulder blades, she knew that was no longer a possibility.

"Then don't act like one," Noel responded as calmly as possible. She got up and walked out the door.

For the next two days Claire left as soon as she woke, and did not return until long after Noel was asleep, if at all. Noel wondered what was the point of Claire's being at this beautiful retreat when she spent half her time escaping it.

She stared at the work before her. Useless. She could rationalize a break. She had been at it since five, even though her productivity was dubious at best. Whatever this grey depression she was suffering was all about, and whether she could label it and organize it in her thoughts, made very little difference to her. She wanted it to go away. An instant twelve-step program. Just add water and stir. Or, better yet, shrink it down to two steps. Get over it. Stay over it.

She deserted her work and meandered out onto the deck. She could always lose herself in the hypnotic rhythm of the waves. She kept attempting to count the seventh wave crest, but kept losing track before she got there. And then a strange and haunting melody fell on her ears. It came from the old upright at Maggie's cabin. Which didn't make sense. Maggie only played after several bourbons and then only rowdy ragtime blues. She followed the music, and then knew it couldn't be Maggie. The touch was too accomplished, the feeling too sensitive.

When she approached Maggie's door, she found herself caught up in a beautiful Chopin Prelude filled with pathos. Nothing could have shocked her more than to see Claire sitting at the old burnished mahogany piano, deep in concentration.

Noel watched Claire's slender fingers glide over the keys, further exposing this unsuspected side of a woman whose facade shunned sensitivity like the plague. She watched Claire with new interest as she continued to play.

Claire stopped mid-piece, played melody with her right hand. Then, suddenly, her back arched. She swung around to catch the intrigued expression on Noel's face.

"Absolutely..." Noel did not want her words to sound cliched. "Alive."

Claire turned back to the piano, shut the case. She looked very soft in faded blue jeans, knit cotton beach sweater, hair loosely pulled back.

"Please, don't stop."

"I'm...finished."

"I had no idea—"

"I had a sensitive side?" Claire chided, "Don't let it throw you."

Noel wasn't in the mood for word games. "What an extraordinary talent you have."

"Please."

"No. I'm serious. I adore it. Especially Chopin."

"My favorite." Claire's tone was wistful, less defensive.

"So deliciously tormented."

"Well, torture is his appeal."

Noel lightly touched a couple of keys. "Is that a particular obsession?"

Claire glanced at her, then away. "Let's just say, it's had its moments."

A gloomy silence fell as Claire's words floated between them. Noel recognized they were both dangerously close to sinking woefully into depression.

"So..." Noel grappled for conversation.

"So."

Noel glanced at her watch.

"You do that a lot."

"What?"

Claire grabbed her wrist, checked Noel's watch for her. "That."

"It's noon."

"Yes. I see that."

"Hungry?"

"Not particularly."

"Me either."

They grinned at the same time. The inanity of the conversation was not lost on either of them. "Want to take a drive?" Claire asked.

"Sure."

****

Claire whipped around a curve at breakneck pace. "Too fast?"

"No."

Claire quickly glanced in Noel's direction. Her profile was implacable as usual. She had an urge to scare emotion on to it.

She pressed into the accelerator and rounded another bend with skill. But Noel's expression did not change. Did this woman feel? Did she anger? Did she lust? Was the containment merely a well-worn facade for a tempestuous inner nature?

Claire wanted to know how anyone could control that side. The dark. The side that was equal parts compulsion and fire. Her own success had been minimal at best. She found herself gravitating towards this woman, so like an anchor, firmly rooted on the planet, while she herself spent most of the time being a kite swept out of the hands of its owner. Claire sped up the hill through a tunnel. When they drove out the other side Noel grinned and turned to her.

"Now I'm hungry."

****

Noel took a gingerly sip of foam off the top of her beer. Claire grinned as she observed Noel, clearly the most out-of-place character in the seedy Humpwhale Inn. A country song wailed from a distant jukebox. Noel's jaw tightened; distaste mingled with condescending amusement.

"She done you wroooo-ooong." Claire laughed as she intoned with twangy melodrama.

"Excuse me?"

"Tore out your heart, shredded it to pieces with her unfeeling faaaa-aaangs..." Claire continued the mock country song, "drop-kicked it into the nearest dump bin, with the rest of the broken he—a-arts."

"How descriptive. You must be a writer." Noel smiled sardonically. "Yes...I can see it in your eyes. Wild imagination. Stormy soliloquies."

Claire smiled in return. She felt very little pain as she took another sip of tequila followed by a beer chaser. "And your eyes, paint a barren landscape, darlin'—sagebrush twirlin 'round your heart."

A shadow of intense pain crossed Noel's eyes.

"Sorry." Claire said quickly. "Sappy music has that effect on me. But you know, Doc, whatever she did—fuck her."

Noel stared into her beer. "Is that your answer for everything?"

"All I'm saying is no one's worth losing your joie de vivre over, Noel." Claire wanted somehow to help her. But as she smiled engagingly at her, Noel seemed to become more uncomfortable.

"So this is where you hang?"

"I never hang."

"No. I rather suppose you don't." Noel took a quick sip of her beer. "What do you do?"

"Oh, I don't think it's any big mystery, Doc. Probably the same thing you do."

"I somehow doubt that."

"Different tools. Same game." They were sparring again.

"It isn't." Noel was direct.

"Isn't it?"

"The attraction between men and women is clear—straightforward, so to speak."

"And between women and women?" Claire teased.

"It can weave..." Noel responded carefully, "dangerously... simply forever."

Claire felt the heat of Noel's pointed directness as the words slid between them.

"Hey ladies!" The spell was broken as Tara, Lynn and Adrienne bustled up to the booth in high spirits. "Mind if we join ya?" Tara didn't wait for an answer as she directed Lynn, who appeared kidnapped, "Come on honey, you just scooch right on in."

Claire looked at Noel. They were unwitting victims. Sending them away was out of the question.

"Looks like we all had the same idea," Adrienne teased.

"Hell yes!" Tara prattled excitedly, "What's the harm in a little bustin' loose, I always say."

"Is that what you always say?" Claire asked, uninterested.

Tara looked at the empty beer bottles on the table. "Yes. That's what I always say. 'Sides...I wanted to see for myself what kind of trouble Maggie was referrin' to." She swiveled to Lynn. "Come on darlin' it ain't the end of the world. You'll get your story done. You've been too cooped up anyway. How 'bout a nice refreshin' spritzer."

Lynn looked uncertainly at Noel, as if she might have the answer. Noel smiled at her, kindly. Lynn buckled. "Well...yes, I guess that would be nice."

****

Several rounds later a live band began playing raucous country rock. Things were gearing up for a wild Saturday night. Claire studied the faces at the table: Lynn, tipsy-toodle and wide-eyed, Adrienne carrying a sophisticated buzz-on, Tara blushing prettily as her delivery became even more accentuated. And Noel, who seemed to withdraw in direct proportion to the increasingly animated din.

Tara screamed over the racket, "Crotch bulge!"

Lynn continued to gawk.

"Well," Tara explained, "we have to have some sort of system to size them up accordin' to our preferences."

"Ab-so-lutely." Adrienne raised her glass of wine. "So tell us about your system, Tara."

"It's not foolproof, of course."

"Nothing is," Claire concurred.

A hefty logger passed by. "Take Mr. Lumberjack, for instance."

They all appraised the tall hunky specimen. "Out of ten?" Adrienne pondered.

"Inches?" Lynn gasped.

"No." Tara dutifully explained as if to a child, "It's just a scale. One to ten. Ten, of course, bein' the largest."

"Seven," Adrienne judged.

"Seven?" Tara implored. "I'd say at least a nine."

"I guess that depends on what you're used to," Claire cut in, and then felt Noel's eyes on her. She wished she had kept it to herself. She didn't need to compete with these women.

"How 'bout an even eight," Tara compromised. "'Course if they're crooked I detract a point."

"And you can't always tell," Adrienne commiserated.

"That's right darlin'. It can be terribly disappointin'. Why several months ago I went out with what I was sure to be an eight, maybe a nine, but he was this short of a five." Tara indicated her disillusionment by pinching her forefinger and thumb together, which sent them all into paroxysms of laughter.

Tara could barely contain herself. Then she sobered up, addressing Noel. Claire was keenly aware Noel did not share their enthusiasm for this conversation. "Why darlin' you look a tad blanched. All this girl talk make you uncomfortable?"

"Why should it? I am a girl."

Claire smiled at Noel's response and held Noel's eyes, sending her encouragement. She was startled when a figure suddenly towered over their table. Brian's eyes glimmered seductively as he moved forward and touched her shoulder. Claire was confused. She didn't want him there.

She introduced him at large. "Everyone...this is, uh, Brian Marquist, another itinerant beachcomber from the Big Apple."

"Ladies." Brian was nothing less than gracious and charming.

Claire watched as Noel took in his dark good looks and

smooth manners and how Noel's eyes left hers when he leaned over to kiss her on the forehead.

"Well do sit down, New York." Tara and her damn southern hospitality. Brian sat.

An awkward silence spread over the table. The exclusive girls club had been joined by a foreign species toppling the balance, changing the tone from easy familiarity to competitive discomfort. Claire had seen it happen a million times from the moment she could walk onto a playground to the subtle and not so subtle sexual politics that invaded every meeting, social or otherwise, which involved both male and female participants.

"See Adrienne, there's more culture here than you thought," Tara ribbed her.

"Apparently. Adrienne—" She extended her hand to Brian. "I'm from the Village myself, and don't mind saying, enormously homesick."

Brian smiled shyly. Tara nudged Lynn as she simply stared at him. "What ya'll doin' in this neck of the woods?"

"Taking care of some business—"

"— Brian is an ethical real estate broker. Tying up a non-profit land deal." Claire felt foolish as she attempted to defend his presence.

"How about a round here?" Seemingly embarrassed at the attention, Brian flagged a passing waitress.

"Southern..." Tara winked at him. "...Comfort."

Claire became distinctly aware of Noel's disgust at this display. She tried to save the situation. "Brian, this is Dr. Noel Benedict."

"Oh. The *roommate*." Claire caught Noel's glance. Brian tried to save it. "You...uh, write, as well as practice medicine."

"Why, Dahk-tah Benedict writes all about the medicine she practices."

Claire slumped in her seat, realizing the situation was

well beyond remedy. Her voice became flat with defeat. "Noel's a psychiatrist."

"Well." Noel put her beer down with finality. "It was nice meeting you, but I need to get back to work."

"Don't let me interrupt. I just stopped to say hi." Brian made no move to leave.

"I have to go." Noel slid from the booth, but did not acknowledge Claire with so much as a glance as she said, "I'm sure you'll have no problem finding a way back."

Claire watched Noel's retreating figure. "Yeah. No problem."

"You hate men."

It was the next morning. Claire had walked out onto the deck with a cup of coffee and, of course, a cigarette.

Noel was deeply immersed in reading a book, and did not particularly want to engage in this conversation. She answered without looking up. "Not in the least."

"But you couldn't wait to get out of his presence."

"I just didn't see any point in staying."

Silence. Claire pondered the ocean as she took a rather exaggerated drag from her cigarette. Noel hoped if she pretended to read perhaps Claire would tire of the subject and leave.

"'What...is...it."

"What?" Noel was irritated now.

"That makes you what you are." Claire's voice was genuine and softly searching.

Noel lifted her head from her book and examined

Claire's eyes. She saw the intent struggle to understand.

"I'm not exactly sure." Noel glanced out at the expanse of ocean.

"So. What's the theory, Doc?"

Noel turned back to her, studied her, trying to determine the origin of the question. "Depends on what makes you feel safest, I suppose."

Claire smiled gently.

"The environment...history of abusive relationships with men, etcetera...genetic, which bears out more and more. None of which matters."

"So...forget the speeches. What do you think?"

"A roll of the dice."

****

The sun dipped slowly as Claire and Noel played backgammon, faced off against each other as they sat on the built-in ledge spanning the length of the window. Noel felt Claire watching her as she rolled the dice and carefully maneuvered her white marble disks. She handed the dice to Claire, but Claire no longer seemed interested in the game.

"When did you know?"

Noel let it rest a moment between them. "Isn't that a little personal?"

"I thought that was your metier."

Noel considered. "OK. What do you want to know?"

"How it started."

"Aren't you curious," Noel stated.

"A writer's prerogative."

Claire's smile was so sweetly engaging, Noel found herself drifting into it, lost for a moment. She cleared her throat.

"I was twenty-seven. She was a...patient." She glanced

briefly at Claire, feeling vulnerable for the first time in forever. She did not want her to misunderstand what had taken place. Then she turned inward, entering a memory she hadn't visited in years. "There was something so engagingly tragic about her. I fell instantaneously. It was, after all, why I became involved with the profession...so I might guiltlessly indulge in my obsession with tragedy and my compulsion to fix it."

Noel paused a moment, being there. "I thought it was the case, you know, that I found so damn fascinating. But I was hooked into her so completely that I found myself rearranging my life for that one appointment: Wednesdays at five."

Noel pulled her knees up beneath her, staring at the floor. "Then one Wednesday, almost an hour late, she walks in. No apologies. She knew I was waiting and that I would continue to wait. That it didn't matter. The funny thing was...she wasn't even there for my help. I never really knew that about her until later. That she was there for me to understand about myself."

A pause. "She was absolutely stunning." There was a catch to Noel's voice. It took some effort for her to regain her composure.

"She walked to the window...like she had the very first time I saw her. She looked out...turned to me. There was a sadness. We both knew she was leaving. Leaving town. She was getting married. She came up to me and said, 'It's better this way.' And then she kissed me. 'Besides, you've lost your professional distance,' she said, and walked out the door."

Claire saw the raw pain spread across Noel's face and a tear slide down her cheek. She frowned, confused. "One kiss?"

"One kiss. I never knew a thing about myself until that kiss. I never knew want until that kiss—" Noel peered directly into Claire. "—what it felt to be utterly aroused. Never understood any of it. Until that kiss."

Claire swallowed, mesmerized by Noel and a new feeling that swept over her so quickly and thoroughly that she wanted to immerse herself in it and in the same breath knew she could not endure the intensity. She broke the frenzied activity racing between her mind and the lower extremities of her body by distancing herself, going to the hutch. She produced a bottle of bourbon and two shot glasses. She needed a drink.

Several hours later they had moved from the window seat to the couch. Claire lounged full length as Noel crouched on the floor between her and the fireplace.

"Don't think the irony isn't lost on me." Claire indicated their stereotypical positions in relation to each other.

"Don't think I didn't plan it this way." Noel mimicked a Freudian accent. "Tell me you zecrets."

Claire turned to her, her eyes serious. "You think I'm a pain in the ass."

"You have your moments."

"Isn't there always a reason? Behavior predicts behavior. I'm sure some shrink said that once upon a time."

"Do you always prefer glib to straightforward?"

Noel's contact was too direct. Claire winced as she sipped her whiskey. "I wasn't always this charming." She stated it flatly, simply: "It takes a whole life time of conditioning to get this caustic, after all."

"You..."

"We all have stories, don't we, Doc? Some are horrific. Some are just plain and simply out of *People* magazine. Mine aren't anything special. It's not like I had it any worse than any other kid from a broken marriage...with a broken mother." Her voice was matter-of-fact. She couldn't speak about her mother without somehow leaving herself, and becoming an objective bystander, sort of how she felt whenever images of the holocaust streamed by in a haunting documentary that couldn't touch her because she couldn't relate to anything that heinous.

"He used to beat her...my mother. Until she was like a boxer, you know, so knocked about...pummeled, it destroyed all her brain centers. I hated her." Claire gulped some of her whiskey. "I hated her ignorance and I hated her for letting him do that to her."

"Did he abuse you?"

"No." Claire assumed an amused tone. "He was afraid of me."

"Afraid?"

"Oh yes. I had already learned about my power, you see. At thirteen." Claire's voice now took on a bitter edge. "It was pure instinct. God knows, I had no verbiage for it. But I knew, I had this power, as sure as I was uniquely female... that men were so absolutely insecure, they were compelled to batter people and things in some primal bleating way..." Her voice softened with compassion. "Like babies having tantrums. But on the inside, they were lost...lonely...pathetic little creatures, forever banished from their mother's breast." Claire was about to take another sip, thought better of it and set her glass down. "And when I knew I didn't hate them, but pitied them, I understood power."

Noel knew Claire believed what she said with utter conviction, just as many of her patients had created value-judgments and their own sense of reality in order to survive their circumstances. She wanted to reach out to Claire, to touch her brow, and tell her she didn't have to be so tough—that her power was as illusory as Noel's patient had been.

An edge returned to Claire's voice. "He knew it and I let him know I knew. Hell, he never laid a hand on me..." Her voice trailed off, empty in its victorious words.

****

Laden with a thermos of coffee, pumpkin muffins, several books, pens and paper, Claire hunted for the knoll she had discovered several days earlier that worked as a perfect wind break. She created a small cushion in the sand, snuggled down behind a driftwood log, and with great anticipation opened the book: *The Naked Truth.*

> The lesbian nation is as diverse as the women who inhabit it. There is an abundant variety and color in this world which engages in dynamics ranging from the butch/femme dyad to the yes/no (push-pull) tango, the top/bottom battle, elaborate S&M dichotomy, to the age-old debate over monogamy vs non-monogamy. There are closet cruisers who enjoy mental masturbation, jockettes, macho sluts, guppies, lipstick lesbians, femmes gone bad, turnabout gals and those who lust for straight women—lesbian vampires, if you will, who pursue seduction and conversion as an erotic device.

"Jesus!" Claire stopped reading, drew a long breath. Again, the feeling from the night before washed over her and she glanced about self-consciously even though she knew the beach was deserted. It took her several minutes to decide how she felt about the words she had read. She remembered stealing into her stepfather's den, rummaging through *Fire Island* and coming across a passage about two gay men. She had the same feeling then that she did now: revolted and compelled. She extracted a cigarette from her shirt pocket, but didn't light it, tapping it against her chin as she continued:

The straight media conjures up the big bad lesbian as a nothing-at-the-mouth Jekyll and Hyde whose only passion is to seduce and convert straight women. For the most part, lesbians are not at all interested in straight women whose ambiguity around their sexual identity leads more often than not to pain and invalidation for the lesbian.

Claire paused again and considered the credibility of the passage. She thought about Valerie, a writer friend who had fooled around with a well-known lesbian producer, had fallen head over heels in love with her, and then proceeded to dump her to return to a boyfriend, an out-of-work actor with bad skin. When she asked Valerie why, she had simply said, "Men may not be that great in bed, but they're a hell of a lot easier on the heart." She had never understood Valerie's decision. She had met the producer, and she was so much more appealing on all levels...

Although the community is as diverse as any subculture, split into political factions and lifestyles, there is always the tacit agreement that being lesbian means not sleeping with men, nor having the desire to do so.

Claire lit her cigarette. She closed the book, leaned back and let the sun seep into her. Interesting.

****

She was blocked. Noel sat at her laptop, twisting her hands together rhythmically, playing with her signet ring. She hadn't gotten a damn thing done in the past hour. She flexed her neck, got up and wandered into the living room, stopped when she saw Claire's bedroom door wide open.

She walked casually to the entrance, poked her head in. She knew Claire was gone. She studied the disorder for a moment. She smiled briefly, thinking that it reflected the machinations of Claire's chaotic mind. As she was about to turn she caught sight of the jacket cover of Claire's book.

Noel felt like a voyeur as she walked over and picked it up. She rifled through the pages. She would put it down in a minute.

And then there is the advent of the lite affair. No pain. No pain. Wonderful in the summer. Has about as much substance as a "blonde joke?" You know—what's the first thing a blonde does in the morning. Goes home.

Noel twisted a knot out of her neck as she flipped *Life Can Ruin Your Hair* over and studied the jacket photo of Claire. Her hair was darker, brandy-blonde, cascading wildly about her shoulders. It worked. The photographer had caught the utter essence of her sensuality. Her eyes, deeply intelligent, probed beyond the surface, and the smirk around the mouth was a sort of tease, as if she were playing a joke on her audience. Noel returned to the passage.

Seriously folks, how are we to expect longevity from a double-cappuccino culture that cannot even endure the length of a commercial? If we just hit the clicker enough times, chances are we will run into something reasonable, even if only for a half-hour. Perhaps a moody black and white...maybe an endearing sit-com... hell, even an intellectual mini-series. But I always set my remote to sleep, and by the time I've awakened the next morning, I've simply forgotten all about it.

Noel slapped the book shut. She intended to put it down but decided as long as she had gone this far she would trespass just a bit further. She took it with her on her way to make tea and nearly collided with Claire who had just let herself into the cabin. It took them a moment to realize they were reading each other's books. Neither said a word, but they both grinned and then continued on their paths.

****

Picking up her mail at Maggie's cabin, Claire sifted uninterestedly through several envelopes. BJ came up behind her, handed her one with Victoria's Secret spelled all over it.

"Hey, when you see Noel, will you give her this?"

"Sure."

"And don't forget tonight."

"Tonight?"

"Yeah...didn't Noel tell you? Dinner at eight." BJ strolled from the room.

Claire read a feminine scrawl on the front and then lifted the envelope to her nose. As she suspected, not so subtly perfumed.

****

"Here." Claire tossed the letter before Noel who was deeply immersed in research.

Noel was perturbed by Claire's abruptness but as soon as she recognized the distinct lettering on the envelope her face closed down.

"Bad news?" Claire hunted.

"No. Yes..." Noel was clearly distracted. "It's nothing."

"Or all of the above." Claire became upset that she could not drive a response out of Noel. "Were you going to tell me about dinner tonight?"

"Hmmmm?"

"Dinner."

"Dinner?"

"Yes. With Maggie and BJ."

"Oh...yes. No. I didn't think you'd be interested."

"Well I am."

Noel got up with the letter and muttered, "Fine," with utter detachment.

"Fine." Claire mimicked. She felt paralyzed, confined by her own boredom and something else. She still had a few hours to kill before dinner. Maybe she wouldn't go. She had plenty of other options. She paced, restlessly, then marched defiantly out the door.

****

Noel sat very still at the window ledge. The envelope rested in her lap, unopened. She considered it every few minutes as she had for the last two hours. She finally tossed it over to the table. Several minutes later she retrieved it. She sighed. Slowly. Picked up the envelope and with great consideration tore it open.

The crunching of gravel interrupted her as a shiny red Bronco pulled up just outside in the driveway. Inside, Claire's figure was barely distinguishable through the tinted window. Brian jumped out and cavalierly met her as she opened the passenger door. He slammed it and then grabbed her playfully to him. They shared a throaty kiss until Claire began to disengage. He pressed for more, leaned into her again. She let him kiss her gently, but cut off any passion. When she pulled away her eyes ran directly into Noel's. A moment of pure shock passed between them. Claire held her eyes several seconds longer, then defiantly pulled Brian back into her, embracing him hungrily.

"You're always getting involved where you don't belong," BJ chided Maggie good naturedly. Maggie grinned at the loveliness that was BJ: warm, sensual, and very female. They had spent a perfect day together. In bed.

BJ sat across from her now, her shining eyes flashing secrets to Maggie as she passed the bread to Claire on her left. There was definitely something going on between Claire and Noel, Maggie decided as she watched them avoid each other's eyes through most of dinner. Claire was animated, but it wasn't natural. Maggie recognized the influence of several glasses of Merlot. And Noel. She was about as much fun as a widow in mourning. Poked at her food. Politely.

"So what's the harm?" Still grinning, Maggie poured more wine into Claire and Noel's glasses. "Cupid is my calling card."

"I know. You'd rather meddle than breathe." BJ turned

conspiratorially to Claire and Noel. "Adrienne and... Tara!"

Claire and Noel finally caught each other's eyes, staring in amazement.

"But—"

"I know what you're thinkin' darlin.'" Maggie imitated Tara as she responded to Claire, "You're thinkin' Tara's got a big southern Magnolia up her butt, but the truth is she's fascinated by, oh, how shall I put this...Adrienne's Northern chaaaahm."

Noel put her napkin on her plate indicating she was finished with her meal, and remained silent.

"I've never seen two people more ill-suited." Claire spoke to Maggie, but everyone knew to whom the comment was directed.

Maggie watched Claire's eyes snap to Noel. Damn fine looking woman, tonight, that Claire, in her little L.A. number. A cream-colored one-piece, snugged sweetly at the waist, accentuated every line of her knockout body, not to mention the V-neck that dipped seductively to the curve of her breasts. Maggie found it fascinating, especially in contrast to Noel's dark blazer, black turtleneck. These two were quite a pair. Oh, the yin and the yang of it all.

"Maggie, you know every time you get into this stuff it turns into one long drama-rama." BJ teased her sweetly.

"I don't have anything better to do." Maggie gulped the last of her Merlot and realized this was more true than she wanted it to be. She stared at the empty wine glass as if it held the answer. Part of her knew it was the answer.

BJ got up and started to clear the table. "Why don't you two go into the living room, while we make coffee and argue some more." BJ directed Noel and Claire as she peered challengingly at Maggie.

Claire picked up her wine glass and followed Noel, slowly. Both of them sat, nestling into several floor pillows by the fireplace. Claire fed the dying embers, adding several dry logs, then turned to Noel, who stared into the crackling hearth, obviously distracted. Claire felt awkward after their distance in the afternoon, and embarrassed by her display with Brian. She wanted to reconnect with Noel, wanted to bring back what had flowed so easily between them the night they had shared those dark parts of themselves. She had no idea about how to make that happen or why she even desired it.

"Quite a pair," she commented about Maggie and BJ. It was a rare occurrence but Claire was at a loss for any other words.

"Yes...They've been coming apart and together for twenty years now." Noel talked more to herself than to Claire.

"How long have you known them?"

"Since I started coming here...five years ago."

"Maggie's a character."

"A teddy bear. Underneath the fire."

Claire studied Noel carefully then, desperate to get under her surface. "And what about you?"

Noel looked at her.

Claire's eyes were open, inviting. "Underneath it all."

Just as Noel's eyes began to respond, Maggie crouched down between them. "So. How's the probe?" Noel's eyes darted from Claire's as if they had been caught. "You know. The intimacy thing."

Noel's relief was apparent. "Oh...well, OK, I suppose."

"Well shit girlfriend," Maggie groaned as she stood back up and ambled to the couch. "Don't sound so enthusiastic."

"I'm just bored with it."

"Kind of hard to write about something you're not experiencing, isn't it?" Maggie needled her.

"I'm sure Noel's sense of recall's just fine." BJ had entered, set down a tray with four lattes on the coffee table.

She gently pushed Maggie to the side as she sat next to her, ran a hand lovingly through her hair.

"So come on." Maggie persisted. "Don't be so goddamn mysterious."

"You're not really happy unless you're bugging me, are you Maggie." Noel was clearly not in the mood.

"I suppose we have to come to your lecture to unveil the eighth wonder of the world."

"Oh, are you doing the artist's series again?" BJ asked. Noel nodded. "Noel's quite the celebrity here," BJ remarked to Claire, as she handed her a latte.

"They don't know what the fuck to think about this very urbane, very sophisticated Professor yakkin' up lesbo sexuality here in our provincial yet open-minded little burg." Maggie pulled out her cigarettes, offered one to Claire. "So come on...give us the preview."

Noel sighed. "Well...first off, the relationship of communication to intimacy is being broadly overlooked, on the most basic level." Her tone became wearily academic. "Most of us are so vulnerable and riddled with neurosis we're not equipped to *really* communicate...without which there is no basis for intimacy."

"No problem." Maggie poked BJ. "You simply match neuroses."

"Equal in all things," BJ quipped.

"Equality has nothing to do with it." Noel's voice was flat. "In fact, intimacy would be far easier if we accepted the honesty of inequality, since there is no such thing in any case—"

"So now equality doesn't exist?" BJ countered.

"Exactly. Let's just be honest and accept it. You like to do this to me and I like it done."

"OK, Doctor," Claire said, accepting this idea, "then what particular Petri dish creates this elusive state of intimacy?"

"The Tallulah Tango!" Maggie bellowed tipsily.

Noel ignored Maggie's crudeness. "Quite often the most direct route."

"So intimacy is only possible during the sexual act?" Maggie noted, even in her haziness, that there was a distinct bite to Claire's tone.

"That is precisely what I am *not* saying." Maggie saw that Noel was reliving an old frustration. They had had this conversation many times. "We're probably more dishonest during sex than at any other time." Noel leaned forward, put her coffee down, and then gazed into the fire as if the answers might be somewhere among the dancing flames. Her voice softened, as she groped for words. "We're all searching...with this insatiable hunger to be intimate—truly intimate, but juxtaposed to that is the battle of how far we will expose ourselves to achieve it."

"What a dreary prognosis," Claire intoned.

"So out with it," BJ said, and then asked at large, "Where do we find it?"

"Different ways. Some of us get it from our friends. A rare few from our lovers. Some of us fuck strangers."

Claire's head snapped to Noel. Maggie saw Noel's awareness that this was a direct hit. But Noel continued, "If we are to be judged, branded, exposed to someone we know, we have to justify what eroticizes us...what moves us. And what if we should want something from our partner that will disgust them? What if what we entertain as erotic revolts them?"

"And what if it doesn't?" Claire was angry now. "Don't you think it's possible to find a meeting of the minds during the act of sex?"

"Great sex does not equal intimacy."

"So you're saying men and women have no hope of achieving intimacy."

"It can be imitated...it can be simulated. But men and

women will never speak the same language. Ergo, men and women can never achieve true intimacy."

"So that rare achievement is reserved only for dykes?" Claire's tone was derisive.

"That would be the logical conclusion," Noel answered wearily.

They were all silent, debating this pronouncement. Noel certainly knew how to put a spin on an evening, Maggie thought as she watched, amused.

BJ tried to save the situation. "Perhaps it comes back down to our lack of language as a whole. Men and women achieve levels of intimacy...just as women—"

"Excuse me, Doctor—" Claire cut BJ dead, glaring at Noel. "—but I think your rhetoric sucks." She bolted upright and stormed from the cabin.

Maggie watched her retreating figure, then shook her head, tsk tsking. "Noel, methinks you have offended the fair lass."

Claire tossed her cigarette over the side of the deck as she leaned against the railing. Maybe it was time for her to leave. She wasn't really getting anything out of this retreat "thang." That probably only worked when you had something to retreat to. Picturesque scenery only went so far. She hadn't found her soul and Salinger had nothing to worry about. When she heard Noel's footsteps she froze.

Noel approached slowly, glanced at Claire's implacable profile. "I'm sorry. About last night." Claire was silent. "None of that was directed at you."

"Wasn't it?"

"It's not a lesbian issue."

"You seem to have adopted it as one."

"It's an issue of communication. Period. You'd think having two women make love you'd manage to have some pretty torrid sex. Truth is, they feel just as exposed and vulnerable..."

Claire was uncomfortable with this dialogue, the two of them, standing there together.

"Like you." Claire shifted the conversation. "Last night." Noel wasn't sure what she was referring to. "The letter."

"Perhaps..." Noel grinned sardonically.

"It rattled you."

"Just...unexpected."

"What happened?"

Noel took a moment. "Nothing that matters now." She shifted gears. "Anyway, I wanted to apologize. Thought I'd buy you a drink at that place you're so fond of."

Claire considered, then decided to let her anger drop. It just wasn't worth it anymore. Being angry with Noel was easy, God knew, but it was also counterproductive. To what, Claire wasn't certain, but she smiled engagingly at Noel's invitation, then turned and led them both off the deck.

****

"I read your book."

They sat in a small booth, listening to yet another ribald tale of country woe wailing from the jukebox. Claire removed a cigarette but didn't light it. "Very enlightening," she said. "Not my cup of tea but it is rather fascinating. Tell me something."

"Hmmm?"

"This butch/femme *thang*. I don't know. Sounds simulated to me."

"You're referring to male role-playing." Noel's academic tone returned. Claire nodded. "In some cases it is. But there is a critical distinction. In our world, butches like to give pleasure. Not take it."

Claire flinched. Noel disregarded it, changed the subject. "I find it so easy to drink here."

"Bars do have that effect." Claire was defensive.

"No. I mean here. At the beach." Noel knew far too well, from a clinical standpoint, about alcohol abuse. Especially with lesbians who had lost their families, their sense of self in a society that shunned them or simply didn't recognize them—the shame, the guilt, grief and humiliation that danced attendance upon their consciousness as they grappled with this new aspect of themselves. How gently the intoxicating elixir lulled the painful memories, anesthetized misery and loneliness, kept intimacy at elbow-bending length. The irony was that it also gave one courage to break down those barriers, as she and Claire were now chipping at their own.

"You think it really has anything to do with that?" Claire's irritation was no secret.

"No...I suppose not." Noel's tone was flat. She studied her hands as Claire studied her pain. It was the pain, so raw about Noel's face, that evaporated Claire's anger. Just when she thought there was something she could really hold onto and use to settle in on a good argument, Noel's countermovements dissipated her momentum. She sensed the intense sadness coming from Noel, and knew there was no relief.

"Hey." Claire put her hand over Noel's and wasn't sure what to do when Noel's unveiled, shocked eyes met hers. She winked, sweetly, then smiled, softly. She removed her hand, self-consciously, then lit a cigarette.

"So what are you working on?"

"This isn't leading to a pep talk."

"Of course not. Come on, what is it?"

Now Claire was the one to retreat into an old pain. "A work-in-progress."

"More jaded views on contemporary dysfunction?"

"Not quite." Claire took a drag off her cigarette, her tone serious. "A novel."

"Hmmm." Noel took another sip. Her eyes sparkled. "And what is this novel about?"

"Sex."

"Ahhh...a sizzling sexualpade?"

"Sure, some of Tara O'Hara's sanitized sex."

"I hardly think that's *your* metier."

Claire's eyes snapped to hers. Noel was baiting her. "What is?"

"Oh, I should say, very rough, raw, down and dirty sort of sex."

Claire considered for a moment. "Well, being a therapist I suppose you have the exact definition of rough...raw...down and dirty sort of sex."

"Yes. It's called fucking."

"Ouch!" Claire belted her bourbon down. Noel's graphic language struck a chord in her. But she wasn't about to let Noel see that. She responded, going for flip, "Sounds like a nasty habit."

"It can be."

"I take it, it's not a hobby." The banter had become deadly serious. "Lesbians do fuck, don't they?"

Noel wouldn't justify Claire's taunt with an answer.

"Tell me...how do they fuck exactly, without the proper apparatus?" Claire heard the angry tone in her voice. She did not want to lose her edge with this woman. Not about this.

"It doesn't take a great deal of ingenuity to figure that one out."

"I've been wondering." Claire continued her attack. "If they're so goddamn well-adjusted, why are they so attached to their dildos?"

"Dildos have nothing to do with penises. It's about penetration, which feels good."

Claire was nonchalant. She had to be. "Sex is sex."

"It may be for you, but sex between women is as raw as it gets."

Claire responded physically. The visual imagery that flew through her mind sent a twist through her stomach. Her jaw tightened. The music faded to an end. There was an empty silence between them.

"What are you doing?" Claire could hear the fear in her own voice.

"Answering your questions."

"This isn't about me—"

"Isn't it?"

"Of course not."

"Then why such potent curiosity?"

"Merely...academic."

"Merely..."

Another tense moment of silence filled the space between them. Claire shifted uncomfortably as Noel's eyes held her.

"What are you afraid of, Claire?"

"If I was afraid..." Claire's eyes were like ice, "you'd certainly be the last person I would discuss it with."

****

Claire's fingers were stiff as she played her singularly favorite and most tormented Chopin Prelude. Restless and tense she pummeled the piano in frustration, exorcising her demons. She knew she was wallowing in a feeling she didn't even have the words to describe, but the more she went there, to this place that burned in her womb, the more she desired it. What "it" was she couldn't ascertain. She had played for hours and felt that if she could simply play until she was exhausted maybe "it" would go away. But the more fiercely the melody wove into her being, the more plagued she became.

She stopped. Her breath was ragged as she stared at the keys. Her hands trembled. She twisted them together and then as if in a supreme effort of decision closed the cover on the keys. She rose, as if by a will other than her own...

****

Noel typed with fastidious concentration as Claire entered her room. She waited in the frame of the doorway as Noel slowly turned to her.

Their eyes locked. Noel stood.

Claire went to her, graceful and deliberate. Within a foot of her she stopped.

Noel slowly lifted her hands to loosen Claire's braid, her eyes never leaving Claire's, every movement punctuated by the clear intent in her eyes. As Claire's hair fell softly to her shoulders, Claire reached for Noel, cupping her face in both hands, and gently kissed her lips. Sweet. Earl Grey tea and honey. Claire's lips traveled to Noel's eyes, her eyelids, brows, down her jawline, cheeks, her chin, to her neck, gently exploring with each caress.

Noel gripped Claire by the shoulders, prying her from their contact, defiance in her eyes. What did Claire want? Did she have any idea what she was doing?

Claire silenced the questions by taking Noel's hands and folding them around her in a complete embrace, then touching her lips to Noel's, her tongue probing parted lips, gentle but determined, engulfed by Noel's essence, clasping her fiercely into her, wanting this and afraid of it.

Noel threw her violently to the side and when Claire turned to her she was gone. Claire regained her balance and moved to the mirror. Tormented, she stared at the reflection, touched the frame in absolute terror, for when she stared into the eyes that peered from behind the magic reflection into her own, they belonged to Noel.

****

Claire's eyes flew open. It took her a moment to get her bearings. She searched for her braid. It was still intact. She bolted upright on the bed, her breathing irregular. She heard Noel's movements in the kitchen. She frantically reached for her cigarettes but the package was empty. She tossed it over the side of the bed in frustration and disgust. She inhaled deeply, cleared her throat.

****

The silence seemed deafening to Claire as she entered the kitchen where Noel was preparing a cup of tea. On the counter next to her was Claire's last pack of cigarettes.

"Would you like some tea?"

Claire shook her head. All she wanted were her damn cigarettes and to get out of the room, but something kept her from approaching.

"Claire?"

Claire brought herself back to attention.

"Perhaps we should consider another truce."

Claire looked at her then. She was bundled in what appeared to be an old favorite sweater, navy blue, with a cranberry turtleneck that brought out the glow in her cheeks. She must have gone for a walk. Her eyes were misted, her hair lightly tousled, and something else. A new softness Claire had never noticed in the tall, impenetrable doctor. Claire found herself staring, unabashedly until Noel became visibly self-conscious.

"What?" Noel said. But Claire was in a world of her own. "What is it?"

"You look..." Then under her breath, "different."

"I'm sorry?"

"Nothing." Claire retreated. "Never mind."

"Claire..."

Claire's eyes questioned.

"The truce?"

"Sure." Claire nodded, slowly, strangely, still inward. "Sure."

****

Maggie sat in the kitchen blowing smoke rings. The others were in the living room pontificating over some extremely important issue, she was certain—right up there with Lynn's recipe for suspense and Tara's next soap-twisted machinations for romance. Maggie nabbed a couple of peanuts, chucked them into her mouth. What was this? Did she hear raised voices? She poured herself more bourbon and rejoined her guests who were lounging lazily about the living room where the debate had begun.

"It's a gift of light."

"It's a sham."

"Exactly."

"How can you *say* that?" Lynn was tormented.

"No...no...you're allowing your intellect to betray your hearts." Shilo sat yoga-style.

One thing for Shilo, Maggie thought, she might be operating on her own set of burners, but she was definitely grounded in her beliefs.

"Romance is a gift of feeling," Shilo whispered, "and no matter how you get there...it's divine intervention. The pure radiance of it all—"

"It's a matter of semantics." BJ's tone was short as she walked up to Maggie and removed the shot of bourbon from her hand. Maggie did not resist or protest. She would merely retrieve her drink later from the coffee table.

"It's a matter of camouflage," Noel intoned.

"I wouldn't expect a pragmatist with your..." Tara

searched with an affected roll of her eyes, "...orientation to think any different."

"You think there aren't any dyed-in-the-wool lesbian romantics?" Maggie sipped her beer chaser, getting back at BJ. "They're the worst. Instead of having just one pining for the white picket fence...you got two."

"Hmmmm...romance to the second power," Claire interjected.

Maggie grinned. Claire had a way with her spicy bon mots. She threw them in when the others weren't looking. She looked quite Noelish tonight, Maggie ruminated, in her black jeans, black turtleneck and cream blazer. Striking.

Maggie watched Lynn, who looked baffled and frustrated. No wonder. The poor thing had felt obligated to wear the tie-dyed body shirt Shilo had gifted her with, and under her mint plaid culottes, besides. Hell, it would mess with anyone's mind. But there was something about her. Underneath all the layers of social right-wing conditioning, there was a spirit, begging to see the light of day.

"You...you always have to do this...you have to tear everything apart," Lynn despaired.

Maggie leaned down to her and said, not unkindly, "It's the only way to get there darlin'."

"We're still being inculturated as women who long to bond...to mate." Noel addressed the group but her target was Tara. "Regardless of our sexual orientation."

Now there was a switch. Maggie watched the ease with which Noel moved in blue jeans and an old black-woolen sweater. Her shoulders were even less postured, less guarded in this relaxed attire. As if somehow she and Claire had stumbled into each other's closets. It worked.

"But straight women are better at boundaries," Tara pouted.

"You're right. However, it isn't a matter of choice. The boundaries are imposed."

"Which is what makes them so friggin' uptight and rigid," Maggie baited Tara.

"Well, I certainly am not." Tara was indignant. "I wouldn't write the kind of novels I do if I were uptight and rigid."

"Then get up, darlin'."

"What?"

"Get up," Maggie ordered.

Tara rose uncertainly. Maggie noticed her own knees were a little wobbly as she moved to Lynn, put a hand to her elbow. "And you." Lynn started to protest then evidently saw something in Maggie's eyes.

Maggie ran a hand through her wild hair as she studied them. She cleared her throat. "You two are sorority sisters, who were best friends five years ago. You've just run into each other at Kennedy airport. It takes a minute to get your bearings. But then you realize, here's the woman that stayed up all night with you while you were huggin' big white with your first kamikaze hangover." Maggie interrupted her narrative to smoothly pick up the shot of bourbon, steal a sip. "You stare at each other. Then big shit-eating grins break out and you go to hug one another." Maggie waited. "Well hug!"

Tara and Lynn hesitated then moved towards each other. Their contact was akin to distant relatives at a family reunion.

"Hell! You were best friends for Christ's sake!"

Claire watched Tara bristle with pride. She leaned in to hug Lynn with more emphasis. Their faces barely wisped by one another, their shoulders grazed slightly as their elbows awkwardly poked out to the side. They parted quickly.

Maggie's smirk, Claire thought, was reminiscent of Alice Kramden on *The Honeymooners*.

"Let's give them a hand, folks. Yep! The ol' Hug-O-Meter reads one point five. Skin contact, twenty percent."

Maggie shook her head condescendingly. "Now. Scenario two. BJ and I..."

Maggie went to BJ's chair, offered a hand to help her up. "We're two lesbians who have met for the first time at a potluck. We've spent the entire evening discussing Martina's utter brilliance, and whether she would have won her tenth Wimbledon title if Judy's timing hadn't been so goddamn premeditated. And now...it's time to bid adieu." Maggie pulled BJ to her.

Claire felt their heat as they enjoyed a full body hug.

While they embraced, Maggie addressed Tara and Lynn. "This, ladies, is Huggus Completus. Note the full body contact." Maggie freed a hand and motioned the length of their bodies. "The fit of our legs."

Claire was riveted by Maggie and BJ's bodies pressed into each other's. As Maggie's words continued, Claire's focus wandered from them to Noel, who was watching Maggie's performance with some amusement.

Maggie's voice was husky as she continued. "We feel one another—the softness, the warmth, the roundness and loving."

Noel caught Claire's glance. She seemed confused by Claire's directness, and Claire, herself, did not understand her desperate desire to maintain contact.

"When we hug it is not something we must quickly repel ourselves from. We fall into it like a down pillow."

Noel shifted her gaze. Claire felt edgy, nervous. "And they just met at a potluck?" Tara would not be the object of humiliation.

Maggie extricated herself from BJ, turned full on Tara who leaned against the hearth. "Now if straight women are so goddamn open and uninhibited, I want to know why they hug like opposite ends of a magnet."

"You've made your point," Tara conceded testily. "Can we get back to the original issue?"

"Yes...please." Lynn was completely rattled.

"What?" Maggie bellowed. "The semantics of romance in literature? Or that throbbing bullshit you write to alienate women from themselves?"

"Maggie!" BJ cautioned.

"No," said Tara. "I'm all for the first amendment. Seems lesbians love to attack my work. I think it's just fascinatin'."

"I am s...sure you do," Maggie stuttered.

Claire recognized that Maggie had stumbled over the fine line between intoxication and drunkenness.

Maggie's eyes took on an unearthly glare as she continued, "It'll probably end up in one of your doorstops, only in reverse, where the straight heroine will convert the poor confused dyke who's been following her on a cross-country rendezvous with some muscle-bound pirate named Blake Swashbuckle."

Tara's lips tightened, but she accepted the lashing gracefully. "There is nothin' wrong with women losin' their dull and unfulfilled lives for a couple of hours in one of my books."

Noel intervened. "Nothing...except themselves."

"We don't want to lose our sense of humor, now do we?" Claire asked them all but her eyes were on Noel. As Noel turned to her, Claire said. "Fantasy's healthy. Right, Doc?"

"If we know where to draw the line—"

"Damn right!" Maggie drunkenly reiterated this point. "Draw the line!" She weaved towards Tara. "Tryin' to clean it up don't change the way it is. Never has. Never will."

BJ caught Maggie as she misstepped and tumbled to her knees close to the fire. Her drunken face highlighted by the dancing flames, she imparted an ancient truth in the inimitable style and graceful verbiage that was Maggie: "If ya eat pussy...Ya eat pussy."

****

Noel was just behind Claire as they entered the cabin. Ever since yesterday afternoon Claire had been acting strange. Distant. Not rude, but different. Diffident almost.

She was wondering about what had caused this shift when Claire stubbed her foot. As she turned to catch her balance, she fell into Noel, right on her heels. They stopped dead in their tracks, so close that Noel could feel Claire's breath. Noel flipped the light on and quickly removed herself from their physical contact.

"She's so charming when she's ripped," Claire offered.

"Yes..." Noel responded, discouraged.

"What?"

"Why is she so angry?"

"Hmmm." Noel reflected. "She's fought a long battle. Women today look at someone like Maggie and they don't get it. Her masculinity...her cantankerous arguing... her need to stand apart."

"She reminds me of the old movement days."

"I wasn't aware you were around then."

"I've done my homework."

Noel moved to close the door. Claire slid between her and it and leaned it shut for her. "Don't you think I know anything about the movement?"

"Doesn't seem like your *cup of tea*."

"Inequality is nobody's cup of tea." Claire felt defensive now. How did this woman always manage to turn it around?

"You don't seem like the bra-burning type." Noel seemed defensive herself. "So how were you involved?"

"On the periphery."

"Well, Maggie isn't a periphery kind of gal. She was in it with both sleeves rolled up, fighting the fight, not just for us, but for straight women as well, and probably every other goddamn cause there ever was." Noel's voice brimmed with admiration. "The Maggies of this world may be a pain in the ass, but without them we wouldn't be where we are today. None of us."

Noel stopped. "I'm sorry. I guess I sort of got carried away." She smiled, embarrassed.

"Do you think it's true?"

Noel was confused.

"What she said..."

"About?"

"The way straight women hug."

"Perhaps an over-generalization." Noel shrugged lightly and walked past her towards her room.

Claire turned off the light, but instead of going to her bedroom, moved to the window. She could barely distinguish the crests of waves breaking on the shore.

"I think it's true," she whispered.

Two days passed before Noel saw Claire again. She recognized a distinct pattern. If they shared something intimate or too real, Claire would make herself absent. Whatever she did, wherever she went, it seemed to be required distancing and when she returned she was again the original Claire, hardened and cynical.

Noel walked in as Claire shuffled through the mail on the kitchen counter at Maggie's cabin. They shared the briefest of glances as Noel moved to the opposite side of the counter and repeated Claire's motion. They were both about to leave when they heard stifled giggling.

In silent complicity they followed the sounds of spontaneous mirth to a back bedroom. Full-fledged laughter bubbled up from the other side of the wall. Claire turned to Noel, then indicated the door, slightly ajar. Noel gently pushed it farther open.

They remained very still and close to each other as they

spied on Tara and Adrienne awkwardly shadow-boxing. But then it became clear they were attempting a body-to-body hug. They apprehensively moved into each other's arms, held each other close. It was a sweet vision, Tara, short and delicately plump, melded with Adrienne, reed-tall, their incongruous bodies warming to each other's. They moved in concert, weaving in the deliciousness of this new experience. Their faces turned ever so slightly so that Adrienne's lips were very close to Tara's closed eyes.

Noel and Claire were as caught up in their moment as they were so that when Tara broke away, Claire stepped backward into Noel, who almost squealed out loud. Adrienne became all business and Tara cleared her throat. Claire and Noel retreated, desperate not to reveal themselves or the laughter floating dangerously to the surface of their throats.

****

Claire counted the seconds it took for the pulpy blood-orange sphere to be sucked into the horizon, so that no trace remained. Several moments after the sky lit up a brilliant violet hue against the darkening blue, Claire realized that she was increasingly bored these days. And restless. Tense. That was the other thing she always was these days.

She wandered through the cabin, picked up a book, set it back down. She leafed through a magazine. She wondered where Noel was. She reminded herself how precious these moments of solitude were, and that she should be enjoying her time alone. Well, she was. She was that kind of person. Liked to be alone. It nagged at her but the single thread persisted: several different scenarios of Noel returning to the cabin. And then what? Trying to escape her thoughts, Claire went to her bedroom.

She sat at the dresser, inspected herself in the reflection

of a large mirrored armoire. She slowly unbound her braid, rotely ran a hand through her freed hair, then stopped. She inspected herself. Closely. She ran a hand back through her hair, feeling the sensual softness of it, letting it caress her as it fell about her collarbone. Her fingers gently touched an eyebrow, traveled her cheekbone to her lips, then trailed slowly down her neck to her chest. She unbuttoned her silk blouse, opened it to reveal her breasts. Captivated, she trailed the graceful narrowed curve between her breasts down her ribcage.

Hearing a sound, she knew she was caught. She swiftly rebuttoned her shirt and composed herself as Noel entered the room. But Noel didn't seem to notice Claire's predicament as she approached, rubbing her temples.

Claire saw the pain in her tightened jaws. "Headache?"

"Impossible."

Claire considered a moment. "Here." She got up, indicating for Noel to sit in her place, but Noel was apprehensive.

"I don't bite." Claire persuaded her to take a seat.

Noel's shoulders were tight, the knots in them holding her at attention. "Relax," Claire soothed her.

Noel twisted her neck, trying to get comfortable.

Claire hesitated, then began to massage Noel's shoulders. She kneaded the spasmed muscles beneath the fabric of Noel's shirt then moved her hands to Noel's temples. Her palms were hot. Her fingers found a life of their own as they gently traveled through Noel's softly cropped hair. Claire swayed, her hands soft and electric, mesmerized. Her breathing quickened as her hands continued to explore. She caught Noel's image in the mirror, eyes shut. Claire's were sweetly veiled with the memory of Noel in her dream, taking down her hair, their lips, barely touching then, with urgency, savagely possessing, Claire entranced, swaying with desire.

It happened at the same time. Claire backed off as Noel's eyes flew open, her shoulders more tense than before.

"Better?" Claire's voice was still ragged.

"Yes." Noel cleared her throat. "Much."

Claire removed herself from the proximity and walked to a window. "I'm bored."

"Yes. I'm stuck myself." Noel adjusted her clothing and began to walk to the door.

"Got any ideas?" There was a quiver to Claire's voice.

Noel turned, but they both simply stared out the window.

****

"Two and two." Noel victoriously stacked the last of her marble disks into the home spot on the backgammon board.

"How about three out of five?"

"Sure."

"Only let's make this more interesting."

"What did you have in mind?"

"How about a friendly wager?" Claire's eyes teased. Noel raised her eyebrows. "The winner gets to drink a shot of Tequila, and the loser..." Claire's voice dropped to a seductive level, "...has to part with a fantasy."

"You're on."

Several games and drinks later Claire and Noel lounged comfortably with each other, playful and giddy. Noel rolled the dice and went in.

"Shit." Claire poured a shot glass of Tequila, handed Noel a lemon, sprinkled some salt on it. Noel downed it, twisted her mouth in bitter response.

"So much for the winner." Noel waited expectantly as Claire hedged. "OK. Out with it. And not some run-of-the-mill housewife masturbation fantasy, either."

Claire mused. Noel watched her retrieve memories and secret thoughts. She was very laid-back in jeans and a soft paisley corduroy shirt, which appeared to be well-worn, a favorite. It was buttoned low to reveal her bronzed chest and what one might desire to imagine. Noel wouldn't let her eyes wander there.

Claire's head fell back as she searched. Her arched neck took Noel's breath away, a perfect blend of sensual and aesthetic. If Claire were stripped of her cynicism she would be, quite simply, beautiful. Shit, Noel told herself, you're just drunk.

She paid attention then, as Claire's green eyes sparkled, and her voice became seductive to suit the story. "OK...It's in a bar. Dark. Smoky. Sweaty... after a day of intense heat... the kind where dirt clods explode when you step on them in the deep of summer...the end of a dancing night."

Claire glanced at Noel, then simply removed herself and visited her own fantasy. "He's standing by the bar. I can't see his face, but I can see *him* from twenty paces. The soul of a trumpet floats in the background...lazy, melancholy, a lamentation. His white cotton shirt drapes over him like a wrung out dishrag. He's hot. Very hot and..." Claire paused, "...hard. The faded shadow in his jeans swells...I walk over...very very slowly, very Grace Kelly, and all I do is cup him. His thighs tense as I feel him straining against the material...the heat in my palm is almost unbearable. I caress, I fondle...gently...sweetly like I was patting powder on a baby's bottom...and before he can say a word, I walk away..."

Noel's eyes were lost inside Claire's. When Noel turned away from her she shifted uncomfortably. Claire swallowed. "Gimme those dice!"

****

"If you're the winner—why am I so drunk?" Noel questioned.

"Ye-es!!" Claire shivered from the taste, let out a rebel yell, then very demurely handed Noel the dice. "Your turn."

Noel was cute when she was tipsy. Not a word one would apply easily to the staid and contained Dr. Benedict. But she was. Cute. She had let go of the need to be utterly in control, and Claire liked it. She was actually quite funny. Claire studied her intently, in that semi-intoxication that allows one to feel without boundary. Noel was incredibly handsome. If Claire were a man she wondered whether she would be attracted to the androgynous enigma, which in one moment made Noel appear strong and assured and in the next soft and female. Would that schizophrenia threaten a man? A woman? Did it threaten her? Or did she find it unusually attractive to have all those components wrapped up in this singularly fascinating woman?

"OK," Noel conceded. "It's in a restaurant... grocery store...a public place. It's the eyes first." Her voice grew husky. "Always the eyes. Something weaves between you...but convention would deny it. You dine with your companion or act like you're reading one of those awful tabloids at the checkout stand...but every time you look up, the eyes are there. On you. Yours on hers. Burning through you. The prickly, almost nauseous feeling of excitement in the pit of your stomach...the welling intrusion...that inexplicable flush of engorgement between your legs."

"You walk to the woman's room. She follows you. You watch...carefully...avoiding those very same eyes. After all." She glanced at Claire. "You might have been mistaken. Then you see her mouth in the mirror. A hint of a smile dips the corner of her mouth, ever so slightly...taunting, teasing. An invitation...so faint, so soft, you're not sure you've heard it. She follows you into the stall.

"She kisses you, first gently...an introduction... then so thoroughly it's like a right...she deftly removes the cumbersome attire, enough so she may indulge in her own fantasy and then her hand slides between your legs..." Noel's voice drifted off.

They were both silent for a long time until Claire inhaled from her cigarette.

"Well..." Claire exhaled with emphasis. "We have one thing in common."

Noel's eyes met hers.

"Anonymity."

****

A man's strong veined hand covers a woman's cupping a bulging crotch. Caressing it. Claire touches the hardened jeans and is confused as it melts into the softened heat of a woman's pelvis. It is Noel, surprised to find herself in a dark murky bar, wispy smoke swirling about her. Claire's eyes meet hers, seemingly from nowhere. She takes Noel's hand, and leads her off into the dark, until they approach a bathroom stall. Two women aggressively maul one another. Disjointed. There are no faces. Eyes. "Always the eyes." Noel's. Then Claire's. Then Noel holding Claire's face in hers, kissing her gently, as in introduction.

****

The next morning they were both a bit hungover. The clear and graphic images of shared fantasies and the vague half-remembered disjointed dreams, of which only the feelings remained, made them both tense, edgy. Claire brewed coffee and then took her mug, sat on the ledge of the window seat, and stared vacantly out to the ocean.

Noel came up behind her. Claire was aware of her nearness. When Noel bent over her, she was taken aback until she spotted the bottle of proffered aspirin. Claire took it, removed a couple, handed it back to Noel. Noel started to move from the room, then stopped.

"Are you going to Maggie's potluck?"

"No." Claire's voice was terse. She softened it to explain, "Friday night. Don't want to miss any excitement at the Humpwhale Inn."

"No. That would be such a tragedy." Noel clamped her jaws thoughtfully, then left the room.

Claire sat, motionless. Goddamn it. It was Friday night and she was going to enjoy herself.

****

Noel walked into Maggie's cabin. Pandemonium had broken loose. Lynn was sobbing, falling apart. Tara, Adrienne and Shilo all rallied around her.

"Her husband," Adrienne explained to Noel, "left her."

"Jesus Christ!" Noel bent to Lynn whose pain was utterly on her sleeve.

"Seems taking care of the kids for the past few weeks has made him realize he feels suffocated."

"It's OK, darlin'." Tara leaned close to Noel, cupped Lynn under the cheek. "You'll be just fine. I know it feels like ya just got kicked in the stomach, but believe me, you do get over them."

Lynn continued to sob. Nothing seemed to help. Maggie approached with a shot of bourbon.

BJ glared at her. "That's hardly going to help." But Maggie ignored her, propping the shot glass inches from Lynn's nose.

"Go ahead honey." Tara nudged her. "It'll do ya good."

Lynn took the shot, gingerly sipping, then gulping the remainder down.

"Much bettah." Tara patted Lynn's knee protectively.

"Now there, you just let whatever's pokin' at your ribcage come out. Better to feel the pain than to keep it all bottled up." Tara extended her coffee cup to Maggie. Maggie smiled and poured a shot.

"Can...can I have some more?" Lynn blubbered.

As Maggie obliged, Noel caught the unmistakable spark between Tara and Adrienne as they smiled at each other in mutual understanding.

"Maybe we should call this off." BJ watched Maggie warily as she gulped down a shot herself.

"NO!" Lynn shrieked. They all stared at her. "I...I couldn't bear..." She looked humiliated. "Being alone," she finished.

Several drinks later an exhilarated tension infused Maggie's living room as the women partied with abandon. The music spun about them, cajoling, heightening, intensifying, building to an electric peak. The more the energy rose, the more intoxicated they became, even Noel, who was just as high but more reserved about expressing it.

"Men are shit!" Lynn proclaimed as she downed another shot like an old pro.

"Not all men." Shilo protectively removed the shot glass from Lynn's hand.

"Aren't they?" Tara jumped in.

Maggie exchanged looks with BJ and Noel. A new Tara was emerging before their eyes. A Tara who had very little to do with the overblown belle of the ball.

"Things are rough right now," Shilo continued soothingly, "but there are many ways to heal. Prayer... crystals. I could recalibrate your heart chakra—"

"Sounds like realignment," Maggie mocked.

"It is in a way," Shilo continued unperturbed, "but it will start the process sooner. Rebirthing might be a good idea too. Then the next time around—"

"There will be no next time around," Lynn declared.

"Sure there will." Adrienne took Lynn's hand, but she addressed Tara more than anyone else. "Come on. Let's dance."

"Go on honey, it'll do ya good." Tara practically pushed Lynn out of her chair, then watched Adrienne's tall figure appreciatively and with a long sigh. "Why is it that men, who have all the power, are so goddamn yellow-bellied, and women, who have none, are so brave?" she pondered.

Maggie, BJ and Noel watched this transfiguration of Tara with interest. "I thought you were the champion of male sensitivity," Maggie provoked.

"That's only 'cuz I want them to be that way. Not 'cuz they are!"

"That may be the goddamn smartest observation you have made yet," Maggie snorted.

Tara dismissed Maggie's comment and, looking directly at Noel as she lowered her girth to her knees, leaned against the table with all their drinks on it. "Maybe you're right. Maybe our language barrier will always keep us adrift, or the fact men always have to up and do somethin' that'll make ya madder than cuss." Tara sighed. "But what if we're not like...you?" Tara encompassed Maggie and Noel as she tiredly pulled her Tammy Faye lashes from her eyes and plopped them into her watered-down drink. "What in the hell are we supposed to do?"

"Some of my best friends are men..." This floated from seemingly nowhere as Shilo lit a joint. The sincere cliché dissipated the heaviness and they all fell into fits of uncontrolled laughter.

The music got rowdier with each passing hour. No one seemed to get tired as the evening faded deep into the night. A sensual beat began; a rock and roll seduction.

Claire of The Moon 129

I knew you well from the moment I saw you there
Wearing your clothes like a locked up cage
What can you see from your throne in the corner
Can you feel this place...

****

Claire sipped her awful martini. They couldn't make anything right in this damn bar. What did she expect from a bartender who looked like he just finished milking the cows. Shit. What was that inane saying—"Wherever you go, well there you are." Claire was never more sick of "there" than she was right now. She was about to order another martini, thought better of it. Brian was supposed to meet her after his dinner meeting. She had waited long enough. She picked up her keys and left.

****

Maggie swung her hips about to the music with great exaggeration.

"Come on Noel, let's dance," Maggie crooned.

"I don't think so."

"Aw come on, strip off that cool professional reserve and get funky, girl." Maggie buffooned.

"No."

"Go on Noel," BJ insisted. "Dance with Maggie or you'll never hear the end of it."

Claire appeared from nowhere. Maggie almost choked on her bourbon as she saw the clear intent in Claire's eyes as she walked to Noel, slowly and deliberately, eyes painted on her. "Excuse me."

But before any of them could say another word Claire grabbed Noel's hand and led her to the floor. Maggie chuckled deliciously. She watched Claire lead with the sensual movement of a woman comfortable with her body and the evocation of dance. Noel danced as if by command. Their eyes were married to each other as the words of the song wove between them.

What do you think I came here for—
Use your head
We're not the same but we could be more
A whole lot more

What could it hurt, to move a little closer
How much pain could one dance be
Could it hurt to be adored for a minute
How could it hurt to be loved by a woman like me

Claire's sensual flamboyancy was a perfect contrast to Noel's economy of movement. They appeared to have danced forever together, their bodies linked in a gridlock of primal melding. The heat between them was electric, and they both let themselves play with it. After all, they were only dancing.

Noel reached out and touched Claire's hair as it grazed her face. Their bodies parted and then like magnets, returned, compelled to each other. The slide of the electric guitar prodded Claire to playfully straddle Noel's leg, in time to the music, shimmying down as she teased Noel with her eyes. Noel responded by clasping Claire firmly about the waist with both hands, commanding the full length of Claire's body to move with her own, their eyes locked together. Noel could feel Claire's breasts brush up against her, her breath, exerted from dance and excitement, burned into her skin. At the last refrain, Claire mouthed the words to the music, then masked her intention after each word was spoken; a push-pull, teasing. The music was over but Claire and Noel were caught in the web of seduction.

"GODDAMN YOU FUCKIN' SON OF A BITCH!!!"

Lynn screamed in agony as her body pressed against the wall, then fell to a muddled heap as she sobbed hysterically, her life shattered.

****

Noel passed Claire abruptly as they entered the cabin, both of them still quite inebriated. She moved to the window, peering out at the black, angry with herself. How had she ever let things get this out of control? Claire's assumption that she could waltz in from the Humpwhale Inn, simply because she couldn't find what she wanted that particular evening, and seek her out at Maggie's, so calmly, so in command, infuriated her. She knew she should simply walk away from this, go to bed, but she couldn't.

"Strike out?"

"Not exactly." Claire was amused. "But you know reality. Such a poor substitution."

"Well, did you get what you were looking for?" Claire slowly walked to Noel, stared at her profile. "No. I didn't."

Noel continued to stare out into the void, then almost under her breath, "Do you even know what you want?"

Claire moved closer. "Maybe you can help me figure it out...Doc."

Noel laughed. "I never tinker with straight women."

"No?" Claire taunted. "Why is that?"

"They take too many straight privileges."

Claire maneuvered herself around Noel so that they faced each other. She put a hand out, coyly touched the hem of Noel's jacket. "But what if they're simply following their destiny?"

"Destiny? I think you're confusing that with fleeting

interest." Noel stared implacably at the unseen waves, unwilling to meet Claire's eyes.

"What about your...oh what was that exotic supposition?" Claire continued her slow circular motion as she moved from one side of Noel to the other, "Ah yes...the Vampire theory, from your book."

"It's not *my* theory. It's an allegory, if anything."

"Whatever. It does have merit."

"For whom?"

"Oh, I think converting someone can be the height of seduction. You pierce the skin, suck the passion from them, leave them wanting..." Claire whispered, "...forever."

"Until things get uncomfortable." Noel removed herself several feet from Claire. The memory of her skin, the smell of her hair, were too close. "The husband finds out, say." She did not look at her. "Opening doors can be very exciting, but Auntie Mame I am not." Noel's words were calculated to pierce Claire's demeanor. "And I never get involved with women who straddle both sides of the fence."

Claire grinned derisively. "Sounds like you never get involved at all."

"If you mean fucking for a quick thrill, the myth's been destroyed."

Claire lost her flippancy. "You think if you just talk about it enough it'll happen, don't you, Noel?" She cut the distance between them as she continued, "If you just wind your little hypotheses and theorems tight enough—distill them to the final intellectual analysis—it'll BOOM!—just happen. Like spontaneous combustion." Claire pressed right up in front of Noel, who turned away from her.

"But you need heat for that Noel. Heat." She moved in closer until Noel felt the full pressure of her body. "You can't even look me in the eye. Can you?" The breath of her words slivered against the hairs of Noel's neck. "You're afraid of me."

Noel held her shoulders tight, and then said with clear warning in her voice, "Claire."

"Don't flatter yourself." Claire turned and left the room.

****

Noel had wandered to her darkly imbedded forest with journal in tow. She found herself there whenever she and Claire got to this point. Except the points kept moving insidiously closer together. She opened the pages, sighed, apathetic and discouraged.

> *She's not ready for this. I'm not ready for this.*
> *Claire's not ready for anything that remotely*
> *smacks of responsibility. She wants to play.*

That's what it is, Noel thought, chewing on her pen. She wants to test the water until the waves get too rough.

> *Her arrogance makes her certain she won't be*
> *pulled in by the undertow. But she's never*
> *played this game.*
> *It might be tolerable if she weren't so damn*
> *incessant and so...so there. That night. The*
> *way Claire moved with me. Danced with me.*
> *Damn her.*

Noel shut the journal in disgust. Well, Claire was a survivor if nothing else. The very art of her survival, the edge of wild inhibition, her irritating chaos, was what made her so fascinating, and the brittle fragility that seemed to envelop Claire when Noel least expected it, pulled things from Noel she didn't even know were there. That was difficult in itself.

She had no frame of reference for this dance. With Erika the feelings were out on the table, hidden secrets notwithstanding. Here black and white was ambiguous and grey—hell, it barely stood a chance.

She let out a long and enduring sigh. No frame of reference, whatsoever.

****

Claire ran until she doubled over coughing. Quit smoking. Quit drinking. Quit all this bullshit. She wanted to leave. There weren't many days left anyway. Why didn't she just go—or, maybe stay with Brian.

Brian. Had she really stopped to consider the options? He was interesting, concerned, intriguing, thought-provoking, sensitive, darkly handsome, and a very good lover. A great lover, actually. If there were ever a time when getting serious should be considered, here it was.

So where was the magic? This illusive romantic ideal. Was it simply a matter of chemistry? She had found him attractive...had wanted to go to bed with him...as she did the others. And then the square-jawed warning from Noel, deep and husky, swept over her from the night before: "*Claire.*" She gritted her teeth, started running again.

She headed towards the rock. She now thought of it as The Rock because it so clearly owned this strip of beach. She approached it breathless, then clambered up the side and sat at the top overlooking the familiar and vast expanse of the bluish tide. How many times could she ponder this same view and never tire of it?

Her breathing slowed, and she slumped back. She stripped off her sweatshirt and let the sun wash over her bare skin. It felt healing, penetrating. She drifted in and out of hazy daydreams for some time then was awakened by a noise below. When she leaned over the rock she saw the top of Noel's head, as she meandered through the path.

"You seem inordinately fond of this rock," Claire said.

Noel spun around, taken by surprise. She finally got her bearings and spotted Claire hunched over the top of the crag. Noel peered up, shielding her eyes from the sun.

"I love its strength," Noel said. "Its solidness."

"Yet it's split in two."

"Sometimes..." Noel was not unfriendly, nor her tone harsh. "That's where strength begins."

They both let the words sink in, then Noel simply walked away. Claire gazed at the waves for a very long time.

****

She contemplated the ceiling, rotely smoking a cigarette. Then, restless, she put it out. Tossed. Turned. Nothing. It was mid-afternoon, and she could not work. She was sick of the ocean, the eternal rhythm of beauty, the endless aesthetic of seascape. She wanted darkness. Oblivion. She turned and studied the wall for a long moment, seemingly spellbound by the orange peel texture.

Almost beyond her own volition her right hand moved to her breast. She stroked it gently above her light cotton blouse, nonchalantly, at first, not really thinking about her body one way or the other. She swallowed, then, closed her eyes. She slowly began to unbutton her blouse. She unsnapped her jeans. She teased herself with a long wait, slowly circling the boundaries of her soft pubic hair, allowing her fingers to caress the hard muscles of her womb, tracing a line to her desire. Her breath became raspy with anticipation. Her lips swelled. And then, the eyes...always the eyes. Noel's deep, piercing, brilliant eyes.

Claire stopped. She could not make love to herself with this woman haunting her every move.

"Shit!" She jumped from the bed, dressed and hurriedly escaped her room.

****

Noel entered Maggie's cabin to find Claire playing a particularly moody Chopin nocturne. Claire didn't see her at first, then sensed her presence and stopped. Noel gestured for her to continue. Claire shook her head.

"Just more torment."

"It's more than that. When you play...it's you."

Claire slumped a bit. She was feeling ragged, and became more weary every time she was around this woman. Her fingers touched the keys. She began another piece, which started out sweetly nostalgic and then crescendoed to dramatic volatility. Noel was fascinated as she absorbed Claire's intensity. Then Claire stopped abruptly again.

"What is it?"

"It's not finished."

"Yours?"

"Actually..." Claire smiled self consciously, "...it's yours. I call it 'The Mystery of Noel.'"

Noel laughed, then her eyes became semi-serious. "What about Claire's mystery?"

"Is that a shrink thing—always answering a question with a question? Or just an annoying habit." Claire's defenses were brittle.

Noel moved closer to the piano, touched a key lightly. "Do you know *Clair de Lune?*"

"Moonlight." Claire smiled cynically.

"An appropriate theme." Noel moved closer yet. "Claire... reaching for the moon."

Claire felt Noel's nearness. She wanted to reach around and wrap herself in it. She wanted to immerse herself in this feeling that grew more intense and intent with every passing moment.

"Play it." Noel's voice was low, soft and insistent.

Claire rose, unsteadily. Noel was behind her. Their bodies radiated into one another's. Claire could not breathe. If she did not leave she would be swallowed into this vortex of energy penetrating her very being, would lose herself in it, drown in it. She wasn't ready.

Noel felt her hesitancy. "Who's afraid now?"

"Great dinner Beej." Maggie smiled sweetly at BJ who poured more wine for Noel.

"Yes..." Noel's tone was perfunctory. "Delicious."

"Oh, yeah. We noticed how you dropped your royal manners and scarfed it right down." Maggie indicated Noel's full plate as she lit a cigarette.

Noel was in a particularly off mood and Maggie wondered why she hadn't just passed on the dinner invitation. But then, maybe things weren't going so well at Cabin de l'amour.

"Leave her alone." BJ began clearing the plates as Noel glanced at her watch.

Maggie watched her like a hawk. "Jesus Christ, Noel, are you ever going to get over that cardboard Barbie Doll?" Maggie felt like a shit as soon as it came out of her mouth. She was never very patient after a couple of glasses of wine.

"Maggie!" BJ came from the kitchen with a pot of coffee. She poured for the three of them.

Maggie directed her disgust to BJ. "It's that goddamn Rita Hayworth throwback! Put the blame on Mame, girl," Maggie warbled, terribly out of tune.

"Maggie, if you insist on crooning old show tunes, learn how to sing, would ya?" BJ was irritated but affectionate.

"Would it surprise you to know she was nowhere near my mind?" Noel's voice was quiet but committed.

"Then what's the problem?"

Noel paused, sipping her coffee. "I'm...tired."

"Right."

"Maggie—"

"For Christ's sake! Maggie this, Maggie that!" Maggie mimicked.

"Let it go." BJ's voice assumed the familiar parental tone.

Noel glanced at her watch again. Even Claire was preferable to sitting here and getting the third degree from Maggie. "Thanks BJ. I should go. And, Maggs, why *don't* you let it rest."

Maggie took the suggestion under advisement, slumped a bit as she continued to smoke her cigarette, a small pout forming on her face as if she were a punished child.

Noel walked to the door. BJ followed her, put a hand to Noel's forearm.

Noel said kindly, "I don't know how you do it sometimes."

"I love her," BJ answered.

"Yes. That's the problem. Despite herself, she's so damn lovable. I know, I know. Detachment." Noel touched BJ's shoulder, concerned. "But she does seem to be getting worse."

"Yes." They both glanced at the floor, then back at each other, embraced in silent understanding.

"Sure it's late enough?" BJ's eyes quizzed Noel, but in a gentle way.

Noel frowned.

"Well, isn't that why you've been waiting? To make sure she's safely tucked in or out of bed?"

****

BJ's words echoed in her brain. Noel was incensed that she had let things go this far. That she had allowed herself to be kept from her own cabin. Yet a part of her knew that she was as afraid of Claire's not being there as she was of her standing before her.

When she opened the door, Claire was domestically tending a fire by the woodstove.

A rush of pleasure washed over her as she entered. "I thought you'd be...asleep."

"So did I." Claire continued poking at the fire, then glanced at her, with something new in her eyes. "But...I didn't want to be rude."

Noel was confused. Claire put down the poker, smacked her hands clean. As she turned back to Noel, a strikingly beautiful woman entered the living room from the hall. Smart, sophisticated, and dressed impeccably but inappropriately for the beach. The woman's lips curled into a seductive smile.

"Erika!" Noel's voice was not her own.

"You've got company." Claire passed them both, glanced at Noel dismissively, and went to her room.

****

Furious, angry, frustrated. Their lovemaking was the union of Erika's longing and Noel's rage. Intense, piercing, and encompassing. Noel was lost in the familiar smells and sensations of Erika's beautifully proportioned body. Erika spent hours making her perfect body a visual feast, and

Noel succumbed to it ruthlessly, hungrily. She had been starving for months, and only Erika could fill her up. She wanted desperately to believe in that as she feverishly rode Erika's unquenchable desire through the night, as they came together, frantic, lost, and insatiable.

****

The coffee grinder buzzed at a fevered pitch. Claire's eyes opened. She laughed at the irony of it. She pulled on a robe and walked to the kitchen where Erika had made herself comfortably domestic as she rummaged about the cupboards.

"Oh, I didn't know you were up." Erika was more than friendly. "Would you like some coffee? Or?"

Claire watched her, feeling unusually territorial as they sized one another up. "Coffee," Claire answered.

Erika poured her a mug, hesitated before handing it to her. "Straight?"

The tension shifted. Erika was baiting her and Claire wasn't sure she cared to engage in battle.

"Straight."

Erika handed her the mug.

"Where is she?" Claire was nonchalant.

"Out rousting up some breakfast."

"I didn't know she cooked."

"She doesn't." Erika smiled victoriously. Claire took her coffee and began to walk away. "Claire?" Claire turned, irritated, now. "You don't mind if I call you Claire, do you?" Erika didn't wait for a response. "You know who I am."

"I have a fair idea."

"I'd like to spend some time alone with Noel. Personal stuff." Erika took in the general ambience. "This cabin is a bit too cozy...if you know what I mean, so I was wondering if you could make yourself...scarce."

Claire's nostrils flared, but before she could respond Noel entered, laden with groceries. Erika sauntered possessively towards her and took one of the bags.

Claire watched them. Not taking her eyes off Noel she set her mug down, emphatically, and walked from the room.

"What did you say to her?" Noel demanded.

"I just asked for a little privacy."

Noel stared at Erika, put the other bag down. Before she could decide how best to handle the situation, Claire whisked through the kitchen and out the door in her sweats, clutching her overnight bag.

"Goddamn it, Erika. This is her cabin as well."

Erika wound her way seductively to Noel, put a finger to her lips. "I thought we had unfinished..." Erika backed Noel against the counter, "business."

"What do you want, Erika." Noel's voice was wary, but her eyes could not mask her desire.

"Oh, come, Dr. Benedict. I thought hidden motives were *your* specialty."

****

Darkened figures shadow-dance in a pale lit room. Claire's face is illuminated in incandescent blue as she stares at the streetlamp through the window. The unadulterated hunger in her eyes shines fiercely as the shadow comes closer, obscured by a cape and fedora. It is a tall stately figure, and Claire knows this is her master. She holds out her hands. The figure walks deliberately to her. Before the piercing ritual begins, that will mark Claire forever possessed, Claire peers into the fiery eyes of the dark creature, and sees a vague image of her captor. It is the most natural thing in the world to her to give herself over to this seducer of the night as the taunting figure plunges into the arched, aching skin of Claire's neck. Claire gasps, delirious with pleasure, a pleasure so intense and elusive, she has only dreamed of it, insatiable and never equaled...of no return. It doesn't matter that her life's source is being sucked from her. All that matters is this sensation and the one that brings her to it. She must see her master. She cannot live until she knows who has brought her life. She recklessly pulls the cloak away to reveal the eyes that penetrate into her own, forever owning her. A slow smile of acceptance passes Claire's lips. It is Noel. She draws the mouth back to her neck. She wants more, and she knows it will never be enough.

****

The tickling, prickling sensation wakened her as Brian grazed her neckline. She shut her eyes. She became sick with consciousness. As he continued to forage and she acclimated herself from the world of dream images she tried to erase the memory of Noel, to let herself feel Brian. She wanted nothing more than to enjoy it. Enjoy him. But the hardness of his body, and the faintly musky masculine smell of ardor repulsed her as it never had before.

"What's wrong?" Brian's voice was husky in her ear.

"Nothing."

But neither one of them was convinced.

****

"Nothing." Noel responded to the slumberous murmur from Erika. Erika turned over and cooed as she rubbed her back along Noel's side.

Noel waited until Erika's breathing relaxed into sleep, then she got up, flung a robe over her shoulders and quietly left the room.

****

Claire swaddled the motel sheet closely to her body.

"What just happened here?" Brian looked confused and disappointed.

"What the hell is that supposed to mean?" Claire was furious with herself and turned her anger on him.

"Shit, Claire, first you're all over me, and then—"

"Look. I don't have to fuck you." Claire saw the pain in his eyes but she couldn't help striking out.

"Yeah...whatever." Brian rolled back to his side of the bed, sighing heavily.

"Yeah..." Claire got up and disappeared into the bathroom. "Whatever."

****

Noel's teeth were clenched as she made herself another cup of tea. Erika had been sleeping for hours and she had been pacing, peering out at the same damn view, running through the maze of anger, disappointment, confusion and denial she could not utter, even to herself. Especially to herself.

A shadow came up from behind her. Erika's hand ran up her arm, resting at her neck, gently smoothing the cropped hair to the side. Noel bristled at the contact.

"Hey..."

Noel didn't respond, continued to stare at the ocean.

"Dr. Benedict, I want to so thank you for sharing." Erika's voice was seductive, then fiercely intense. "It's always so good with you."

Noel's body was straight and unyielding.

"I could taste it, Noel. I've waited too long." Erika finally sensed that Noel was a million miles away. "What's the matter? You were there with me."

"I..." Noel wasn't sure what to say. "It's..."

"Certainly the great communicator can come up with something better than that." Noel studied her a moment, her eyes piercing through her. Erika's insecurities hung like shredded ribbons on her sleeve. They always had. She just used to be much better disguising it. Erika had always been an open book. Noel looked beyond her, then, knowing her hunger for this woman had been an illusion. Erika had been an illusion from the start.

"It's what I want." Erika tried a different tack. "It's all I have ever really wanted."

Noel's jaw clenched in disgust. She twisted her body away from contact and moved several feet, never taking her eyes off the ocean.

"Have you bothered to tell your husband that?"

****

"Poor darlin'." Tara sipped her tea. "I put her on the bus this mornin'. Her life's goin' to be utter hell for the next few months."

Maggie drank her coffee. BJ had convinced her to stay on the wagon for a week. Hell, she could give it one week. She looked around at the women who had spent the last four weeks of their lives there. They were silent, feeling Lynn's pain, a condition they had all been in at some juncture in their lives. This was the last meeting and an air of nostalgic solemnity filled the room.

"Well, ladies...this is it. Our very last Thursday night soiree! Bet you'll miss them." Maggie grinned. They all chuckled. "I know I will."

"How about some sincerity." BJ came up behind her. "Just once, dear."

"Surely you jest. Let's see. Sincerity. OK. It's been an interesting group this year. Some heated debates, broadening of the minds...couple of intriguing turns...in the most unlikely of places." Maggie's eyes buzzed from Tara to Adrienne, and then rested momentarily on Claire. She peppered her next statement with innuendo. "Some fun, and hopefully you all got what you came for. Only have two openings left for next year. You can count on one thing. Each one's more fascinatin' than the last."

"Well if it's such a chore, Maggs," BJ teased her, "why in the hell put yourself through it?" BJ pulled her close.

"Not in front of the children, dear."

"If you eat..." BJ mimicked, seductively.

"She says this now, but as soon as she gets back to the city she'll revert to her uptight, anal ways." Maggie wrapped her arms over BJ's. She would always adore this woman who put up with her. She felt lucky, suddenly, even if a bit hungover.

"Take it while you can." Shilo's voice floated over them all. "Take it while you can."

****

Noel and Claire walked from Maggie's cabin several paces away from each other. At the cabin they immediately retreated to their rooms.

Claire packed her clothes. Noel discarded the work before her. She heard Claire in the kitchen.

Noel hesitated. She walked out and saw Claire had stuffed the last of her belongings into an overnight bag that sat precariously on the counter. Claire pulled out an opened bottle of wine from the refrigerator, poured herself a healthy glass.

"I'm sorry." Noel's voice was void of emotion. "She had no right to ask you to leave."

"Well?" Claire studied Noel's face, the guilty expression on it. She popped the cork back into the bottle of wine with emphasis. "I guess misery's better than nothing."

"It's over." Noel's eyes were full of pain.

Claire felt the rawness in Noel's voice. It ripped into her stomach and immediately turned her anger to compassion. Her impulse was to reach out to her, but she couldn't. She had no control these days over her feelings, or what she wanted to do about them. She felt like a crazy woman. She trusted nothing, no one, least of all herself.

Noel mechanically touched the robe that half fell out of Claire's bag. "Going...somewhere?"

"Yeah."

"Oh."

"And I thought, since there's only a couple of days left. I might as well stay with him." Then, as an afterthought, "Brian."

Noel fingered the edge of the robe a second longer. "Quite a commitment, isn't it?"

"I'll live with it." Claire took another gulp.

"Claire. It isn't necessary for you to leave."

"Hey, no problem. I've just made other plans."

A long silence passed between them.

"I guess that's it then." Noel said goodbye with her eyes and walked out the door.

Claire's jaw tightened as she finished off the wine. She closed her eyes. It hurt. But then, she was used to pain.

****

"I've been watching you." Young, brash, generically studly, he was a kid in his early twenties.

"That supposed to make my day?" Claire exhaled throatily.

"It's just you've been lookin' so miserable, I thought I'd come over and cheer you up."

Claire's facade dropped over her like a well-worn veil. "You did, huh!"

"You betcha." The kid indicated another round to the bartender.

"Now isn't that sweet."

"You like to dance?"

"Depends." Claire was already bored with this familiar descent into the mundane.

"I studied movement in school." He rattled on, unaware that Claire was completely distracted. "Movement and acting. Coach says it's for sissies—swears I can make it on a football scholarship, more dignity in that ya know—but I'm no yo-yo. I can make a lot more modeling..."

His voice faded into the relentless country twang rattling out of the jukebox. Claire studied an image of a woman who was long familiar with small talk, the aimless and animated chatter that led to the conquest and conquered. It stared back at her from a mirror lined with Tanqueray and Smirnoff, the face filled with boredom and loathing. What had changed? She glanced at the kid, merrily chatting away to himself, completely self-enamored.

Abruptly she twirled her bar stool towards him. "You know what, Joe College?" Claire tossed her cigarettes into her purse, slinked off the stool. "I'm sick of this place."

Paydirt! His eyes were fire. And he hadn't even had to try. Yeah...modeling for sure. He downed his drink, eagerly tossed some money on the bar and started to follow.

Claire threw her purse over her shoulder almost hurling it into his perfect aquiline nose. She barely acknowledged him as she made her exit. "And I don't need any company."

The air went out of his tires as she stumbled forward. She walked uncertainly forward. Dizzy. She had to get out of there. Escape. She knocked against several people on the way out of the crowded bar and then into Brian as she neared the exit. Awkward tension swirled around them mingled with the heavy smoke.

"Small world." Brian grinned uncertainly. "Hey, you still don't have to fuck me... but how about a drink?"

Claire had already had too many drinks. In her lightheadedness she watched Brian's gentle smile. He was sincere, sweet, vulnerable. She touched his chin, leaned up and kissed him.

"Ah..." Brian sighed, "You must be a Scorpio." Claire's smile was self-deprecating. "Claire..." He leaned closer peering directly into her eyes. "I can rearrange things. Stay a few extra days."

Claire considered a moment, still hazy. "I thought ..."

Brian stopped her with a passionate kiss. "Come on. Let me buy you a drink."

"Sure."

He began to lead her back to the bar, but she stopped in her tracks.

"Claire..." His eyes pleaded. "You know something's here..." He waited, his face hopeful, uncertain. "Just give me half a sign."

Claire considered him, hazily, but even in her drunken confusion she knew there was only one place for her to go. "I can't."

****

Claire paced her empty motel room. She had spent the night pacing. Her head pounded, her throat was dry, the fury of her hangover plagued her body and soul. It was three in the morning. She had left the bar, found a shabby room, and had lain on the bed staring at the ceiling until the alcohol began to recede and her mind furiously jumped into activity. Now as she paced, she began to rehash her entire stay at this damn writers retreat with the most absurd collection of women ever gathered. A sitcom. She could pitch it to Ben when she got back. Especially her and Noel. The veritable odd couple. Yeah, that would go over well on prime time.

Her mind raced for hours. Between her sardonic overview of the past four weeks and the throbbing in her head, she was near migraine. She took some aspirin and drew a bath. She soaked for an hour, the frantic activity of dazed neurons soothed by water so hot and punishing she could barely tolerate it. Soak out the alcohol. She sat in the room. She waited until dawn and headed to the beach.

She wandered for miles, but nothing could still the nervous energy pumping through her veins. She ran. She ran from the memories of the past fifteen years, from the life she had so securely placed herself in, autonomously in control, sustained by an illusion of never needing anyone. She ran to escape her loneliness, her demons, her failures. But they followed tight on the imprint of her soles on the sand. She stumbled. Her body no longer had the strength to run. Her soul was tired of running. She had run all her life.

And now she was at the end of it. It was strange how it happened. You came up against yourself one too many times and it was over.

She couldn't feel the cold of the water as the waves washed over her body. She could only wonder, dumbly, at the betrayal of her physical being to succumb to the icy undercurrent. That would be the ultimate end to this race. Her body was void of feeling, the freezing water lapping against her thighs, as casual as lotion being spread over her limbs. She could feel her flesh against the sand, her bent knees torn by the gritty grains. And in that moment, she knew if she did not move soon, she would not move at all.

****

Noel bent her head into the cutting wind as she stumbled against the gale force. An angry dark blue gray loomed ominously on the horizon as the storm teased its way up from the sea. Frightening and exhilarating. The perfect back-drop for her mood. It would cleanse her. From Erika. From...Claire. Claire, who crept insidiously into the perimeter of her consciousness, taunting, cruel and relentless.

She headed to the rock. Her rock. If she made it through the torrent of wind she might find some measure of solace. She wasn't sure how, but she held the hope that its strength would feed her.

She dodged the rushing tide as she jogged to the west side of the crag several hundred feet before her. She continued on, steadfast, the whipping gusts throwing her body off balance.

****

Claire stumbled towards The Rock, with a sense of purpose she did not begin to understand. She held her body upright as she rounded the east side.

When she approached its broken core she saw her.

In the same instant Noel became aware of Claire.

Noel entered the heart of the crag. Claire tripped towards her on her path, and fell into her from sheer impact of the wind and the rough sand shifting about her feet. Breathing as if for life, her eyes angry at the final betrayal of her old self, she reached out, grabbed the back of Noel's neck, pulled Noel's lips to her own, savagely, impatiently, hungrily. Noel clasped Claire to her as their embrace lasted an eternity, filled with the anguished longing of hours, days, endless moments of desire, pain and rage.

Claire pushed herself away. They were both shaken. "That's because...I...will never see you again."

****

Noel packed the last of her equipment, bags, books, as Amy shuttled the remainder of the boxes to the car. Maggie strolled in, and leaned against the frame, watching Noel carefully. Noel deflected any memories as she moved abruptly past her out onto the deck.

Noel noticed Amy waiting patiently by her side. "Yes?"

"Do you want the Oxburg material for your lecture?"

"No. I don't think that will be necessary." Noel dismissed Amy and attempted to get past Maggie without any speeches.

"BJ and I will be there. At the lecture."

"Great."

"Amy looks different."

They both glanced at the transformation. A long flowered skirt, gargantuan purple sweater and baby's breath adorning her hair had replaced the fastidious attire of several weeks earlier.

"She's been working for a colleague. Ex-hippy, liberal from Reed."

"Ahhhh." Maggie chuckled, then turned a concerned frown to Noel. She knew Noel was suffering. She only wished she could absorb some of her friend's pain. Damn, life was a bitch. This sober shit wasn't much fun either. But the sex. Un-fucking-believable. "You know how I can be sort of a shit when I get to feeling loose. I'm sorry. About Erika, although I'd guess that's not exactly the primary concern on your mind—" Maggie shuffled, not sure what to say. Her eyes were kind and serious. "Why don't you stay awhile. BJ's going back to the city. We can spend some time. Hell, I can...oh, I dunno—"

"Maggs!" Noel turned to her, smiled. "You are the biggest pain in the ass."

Maggie shrugged with acceptance. She was.

"...The irony being that by not allowing ourselves to be integrated into the mainstream we are exercising the most paradoxical form of homophobia. Afraid we will lose our sense of identity by allowing any of our subculture to fit in. Fitting in is not a crime. The political factions demand we take a stand and be quote, other...with the same rights. It is admirable and I applaud lesbians who carry a banner and wave the Lesbian Nation's flag over their heads. But there are other women who desire to be lesbian, and love women, and still integrate themselves in a way that makes *their* lives full. Let's remember a common theme of many of our marches in the eighties. 'Unity in diversity.'"

The applause was resounding. Dr. Noel Benedict searched the blur of faces filling the auditorium. Someone escorted her offstage and took her to a lobby where she began signing her latest book, *The Politic of the Politically Incorrect Lesbian.*

Noel scanned the eager faces as she put pen to page. The line was interminable, and the drain of answering the same endless questions put her on autopilot. All she could think about was getting the hell out of there.

****

She went back. She didn't know why. Maybe she thought being there would ease the pain. Maggie might be right. Maybe she was simply being masochistic. She didn't care. She was tired. Exhausted.

She slept. Dreamt. Hazy dreams all jumbled, scattered, Erika drifting in and out, Maggie warning a gale storm was on its way in. Noel needed to leave. The storm would swallow them up. But she couldn't. She had to find the lighter. Claire's lighter. Claire floated in, in bright vibrant colors, like the painting in her room, larger than life. Even her skin tones were deep royal blues flanked by magenta and indigo shadows. They were entwined in each other's arms lying on the beach near a fenced sandbar, as if they were the star-crossed lovers out of *From Here to Eternity*. The giant tidal wave lurking in the background suddenly rushed over them and carried Claire out to sea. Noel's arms were empty as Claire's hair, a brilliant shimmering gold, washed away in the waves, never to be seen again. It was like an ancient Grimm's Fairy Tale in its surrealism, and left her feeling empty. And terribly lost.

She thought about the dream now as she sipped her tea. Well, some things never change. But she had. The pain of Erika was gone. The pain of Claire had replaced it, she thought ruefully. But it wasn't the same kind of helpless, senseless pain. She loved Claire. She loved her for bringing Noel back to a part of herself that had left the day her mother died: her fire. In all of its vagaries, moods, dramas and pitfalls, life was exciting, and though she'd told her patients a million times nothing was ever gained without risk, it was Claire's ability to incite emotion, raw and untamed, in all her humanness, that had pumped life back into her veins. She would always love her for that. It didn't even bother her pragmatic mind that she was being uncharacteristically romantic about the whole unrequited "thang" as Claire would call it. It simply was.

****

Hours later Noel shifted her position. She had sat at the window reading, and then drifted off again into another dream she couldn't remember. Something had awakened her. She stretched and got up. She had left the lights off. The dark felt peaceful and safe. After several moments she wandered into the bedroom and lit a fire and warmed herself against the setting chill.

She heard Maggie's footsteps on the deck and then the door open. Probably coming to check up on her. She loved her wonderfully cantankerous friend, but what she needed was solitude. Noel stoked the fire and turned to greet her.

But it wasn't Maggie. Someone moved cautiously in the darkened shadows.

It was Claire.

Her stance was nonchalant, although her being there was not a casual remark. And she was different. There was a softness in her gently pleading eyes. Her hair appeared a silvery golden in the moonlight, wrapped partially back in a Desdemona braid that brought out the fullness of her Renaissance beauty, beguiling and magic. Noel could merely stare at the ghostly apparition before her, fearful of making a move lest it evaporate into thin air. But she was real.

Claire could not move. The endless moments they had faced each other off flooded her mind. She did not know how to approach this woman, how to span the chasm of fear.

Their eyes struggled as they assessed one another, wary opponents.

Noel watched Claire assume an old air of defense as she walked to the bed. She threw Noel's new book on it. "You forgot to sign this."

"Don't."

"I was there." Claire's voice betrayed this incidental information. "I didn't want to be. But somehow...I ended up there." A twitch developed by her eye. She rubbed her forehead in frustration, attempting self control, but there was none, and she knew it. "Just like I ended up here."

Her eyes penetrated Noel's, direct, full of heat as she moved towards her, barely able to maintain her breathing, ragged, sharp, intent. Noel put a hand to Claire's face to help steady them both. Claire grasped it in her own and pulled Noel to her as they tumbled onto the bed.

Claire greedily enveloped Noel in her arms, struggling against the confines of human movement, tearing at her, hungry, injured, impatient, wanting only to have her inside. Noel's lips parted, trembling, desperate to feel Claire's tongue, her soft wet lips as her mouth bruised Claire's with need, ravaging without boundary. Noel's hands swept to Claire's hair, her fingers shaking, mercenary in their mission.

The contact was too intense to bear. Noel stopped. Dizzy. Desperate to regain control but their momentum was already a beast of its own making and swept them forward.

Claire's hands clutched Noel's face, aching to touch her jaws, then turned Noel's face commandingly so that Noel was directed to Claire's arched and exposed neck. She wanted Noel to take her, to hurt her, to mark her, to quell this agonizing need in her. Noel's teeth plunged into the gracefully curved muscles, as Claire screamed, raw, anguished at the impact of pleasure pouring over her, infusing her, igniting the flame, the essence of desire.

Noel's mouth traveled to Claire's. She stopped. Her arms trembled as she pushed herself away so that she could look into this woman's soul who had tormented her beyond pleasure.

Claire returned the penetrating gaze. "I've waited so long."

"Forever."

"Forever." Claire could barely utter the words as their lips met; an interminably engulfing embrace, searching, then frenzied, consuming.

Claire tore at Noel's clothes. She needed to feel her skin. It was beyond reason. When her bronzed skin touched Noel's smooth sinewy flesh Claire felt as if her skin would melt into Noel's by osmosis, their bodies gripped in sacred union. Claire pushed Noel to the side, moved on top of her, painting her body on Noel's as if it would be her last act. Then it began. Deep. So deeply buried inside her, it ravaged to be free. Her body spurred by the compelling hunger within, gained momentum, urgent, escalating, grinding into Noel with primal need, gasping, trembling without control as she came swiftly, without warning, simply from the impact of being with this woman. This woman. She embraced the sweet explosion of her senses, grasping Noel to her as Noel shuddered in the same exquisite moment.

****

The warmth of Claire's mouth. Her full lips, her tongue against her own. The heat of her skin. Her smell. The light acrid-sweet linger of cigarettes married to her perfume. Sensual. Alluring. Noel's palms tingled on the fine-toned skin, as if she could feel each separate hair on this woman's golden-tanned flesh.

Noel's stomach twisted, aching sweetly as her lips explored every nuance of Claire's body, as her mouth traveled, memorizing every contour, the dip from her quivering ribcage to the flat plane of her stomach, the curve of her hip, her solid muscular thighs, waiting until she could hold off no longer.

Wet. Exquisitely wet: the truth of desire. Hot. The taste of Claire. The swollen sweetness. The tenseness as she arched and Noel felt Claire peaking. Wracking. Claire's body convulsing gracefully as she came. Hard. And again.

Claire's hands reached for her and as her body lay upon Claire's, their bodies breathing as one, Noel knew she had finally come home.

Claire's lips. Upon her mouth. Her eyelids. Claire bit her jaw as she gently pushed Noel to the side. Her hair cascaded upon Noel's face, shrouding them in silk. Claire's tongue upon her breast now, teasing her...she was always teasing her, and now her fingers, lightly upon her nipples, and she thought of those same fine hands dancing on the keys, as they now played her, commanding, demanding her until Noel thought her body would explode if Claire's mouth did not find her soon.

And when her tongue fed Noel's hunger, her body filled with uncontrollable arousal, the light pierced behind Noel's eyes, as she came, came without shame at her desire for this woman, who shattered all restraint and brought her to the core of her fire.

Claire's eyes were filled with wonder before her lids failed her in renewed desire. Noel continued to make love to her in a way Claire had never experienced. How could anyone be so assertively gentle, arouse such intensity of feeling, touch her in a way that was so innermost female? Noel was right. About intimacy. The things she had said. But Claire could no longer attach thought to this new experience, as she neared orgasm again...closer...closer, so near, now, the blackness in her head almost overcame the pleasure of her body...closer, oh, God, now, "I'm coming, Noel...I'm coming for you."

****

"Claire...Claire...Claire..." Noel chanted as if in mantra, reverence. Their eyes locked as Noel penetrated, thrusting gently now, feeling the receding waves of Claire's orgasm. Tears fell from Claire's face. Tears of release, joy and fulfillment, as their angry passion was finally spent, and their loving had taken a new form of expression. The movement of their bodies, was slow, entwined, languid and unhurried. They explored with eager excitement, but with an intensity that would merge them forever. "I love you, Noel."

Noel's eyes were bright with loving tears. She kissed Claire softly, lingeringly in answer.

"I love you, Claire."

Nicole Conn – Writer/Director/Mother

Nicole Conn has been a die-hard romantic and black and white film fan from the age of ten.

Her penchant for adult and dramatic story telling is evident in her latest feature film, Elena Undone touted as "sexy and smart and smoldering." This classic romance with a twist, also hosts the Longest Kiss in Cinema History, a claim veteran lesbian writer Nicole Conn's (Claire of the Moon, little man) is thrilled to be held by two women.

Conn's previous venture, little man, is a documentary she wrote, directed and produced about her own premature son born 100 days early and only weighing one pound. The feature documentary went on to win 12 Best Documentary Awards, along with the prestigious Cedar Sinai's Courageous Beginnings Award and Family Pride's Family Tree Award. The film made three TOP TEN FILMS OF 2005 list and Showtime picked up the feature and ran an Emmy campaign on this hard-hitting story about Conn's son's premature birth and subsequent 5-month hospital stay in a Neo-natal Intensive Care Unit.

In efforts to continue her support of other parents who find themselves thrust into the insanity of the NICU, Ms. Conn collaborated with Preemie Magazine Founder Deborah Discenza in creating the The Preemie Parent's NICU Survival Guide: How to Maintain Your Sanity and Create a New Normal published in January, 2010.

Conn's passion for film carried her through her first feature in which she raised the money, wrote, directed and produced Claire of the Moon, the maverick film about a woman's journey to her sexual identity. The film garnered rave reviews and paved the way for lesbian themed cinema in 1991. Conn also created a FIRST for lesbian cinema: ancillary in the form of a novelization (in its 15th reprint and 10 Year Anniversary Republish) a making-of documentary MOMENTS (best-selling lesbian documentary ever made), soundtracks, posters, t-shirts, etc. She followed these projects with the award winning short film, Cynara... Poetry in Motion.

A two book deal with Simon Schuster produced the novels, Passion's Shadow (1995) & Angel Wings (1997), a new age love story. The script adaptation for Angel Wings won the 2001 Telluride Film Festival's Best Screenplay Award. In another pioneering effort, The Wedding Dress was chosen by AOL Time Warner for its new internet endeavor ipublish, which debuted in June 2001. She Walks in Beauty was published in September, 2001 and is currently in development as a feature film along with several other original screenplays Conn has penned.

Conn achieved industry recognition with her film Claire of the Moon and was a finalist in the prestigious Academy of Motion Picture Arts and Science's Nicholl Fellowships in Screenwriting. She believes in giving back to the community and sponsored the Claire of the Moon Scholarship in 1998, awarding second time novelists through the ASTRAEA Foundation.

Well known for her speed, quality and prolific ability to write in many genres, Conn has written five novels, a parent's guide, two teleplays, eleven screenplays, and has produced four soundtracks.

She is currently in post production on "A Perfect Ending," her next feature which she wrote, directed and edited through the film company Soul Kiss Films (Empowering Women One Film at a Time) co-founded by she and her life and film partner, Marina Rice Bader. Ms. Conn resides with her life partner, Marina and their family of six (wonderful if precocious) children in Los Angeles.

Best Feature – "Elena Undone" -Audience Award, Reel Pride, Fresno

Best Feature – "Elena Undone" Tampa GLFF

Best Documentary Audience Award, Los Angeles Outfest – "little man"

Best Documentary Jury Award, New York NewFest –"little man"

Best Documentary Audience Award, San Diego Film Festival –"little man"

Best Documentary Jury Award, Chicago Indiefest – "little man"

Best Feature HBO Audience Award, Miami GLFF – "little man"

Best Documentary Jury Award, Philadelphia Int'l GLFF Film Festival – "little man"

Best of the Fest Award, Indianapolis G&L Film Festival – "little man"

Best Documentary – Jury Award Chicago Reeling Film Festival – "little man"

Best Documentary – Glitter Award – LA – "little man"

Best Documentary – Long Island G&L Film Festival – "little man"

Best Documentary - WA DC – Reel Affirmations – "little man"

Palme D'Or – Reel Pride – "little man"

Telluride Film Festival's Best Screenplay Award – "Angel Wings"

Courageous Beginnings Award – Cedars Sinai, Los Angeles
Santa Barbara Social Justice Award Nominee
Academy of Motion Picture Arts and Science's Nicholl Fellowships in Screenwriting.